CANNIBAL LAKE

CANNIBAL LAKE

A Thriller

Andy Gregg

Five Star • Waterville, Maine

Copyright © 2003 by Andy Gregg

This novel is a work of fiction. Names, characters, places and incidents are either the product of the author's imagination, or, if real, used fictitiously.

First Edition
First Printing: September 2003

Published in 2003 in conjunction with Tekno Books and Ed Gorman.

Set in 11 pt. Plantin by Liana M. Walker.

Printed in the United States on permanent paper.

Library of Congress Cataloging-in-Publication Data

Gregg, Andy.
    Cannibal Lake : a thriller / by Andy Gregg.—1st ed.
      p. cm.
    ISBN 1-59414-059-6 (hc : alk. paper)
    1. Inheritance and succession—Fiction. 2. Indians of North America—Fiction. 3. Missing persons—Fiction. 4. Vacation homes—Fiction. 5. Land tenure—Fiction. 6. Wisconsin—Fiction. I. Title.
PS3607.R48C36 2003
813'.6—dc21
                           2003049238

This book is dedicated
to the people of the Hayward, Wisconsin, area.

Chapter 1

We're All Cannibals

Uncle Roland went missing in January.

The old scholar had disappeared from his lonely cabin on wild Windigo Pond in the Wisconsin North Woods. The lake was named for the Indians' legendary cannibal monster, and Roland had vanished as completely as if one of those creatures had eaten him.

He hadn't been seen for weeks. His Indian friend, old Charley Rogers from the nearby Buckskin Reservation, had come to visit and found the cabin door unlocked, the frozen remains of a supper on the kitchen table, and no human footprints in the fresh snow outside.

Jason Targo wished he could have been up there to help look for his uncle. But when it happened, Jason was recovering from a bullet wound. Now, in the middle of summer, exercise had built up a body thinned by time in the hospital. Some muscle now covered the damage, but he sometimes still felt stiffness and pain.

He glanced at his watch, then at the Honda's odometer. After an hour of driving, he was still about three hundred miles from the cabin. The soothing sights of green fields and darker green trees beside the highway didn't distract his thoughts.

His Milwaukee apartment was closed, the rent and utilities paid in advance. A burglar wouldn't find anything worth taking. The safe deposit box held any important papers, the .38 Police Special he'd worn on his belt for years, and the smaller .32 automatic he'd stuck in his hip pocket when he was off-duty. He wouldn't need the guns for a while, just as the force wouldn't need him until his back was okay. And thank God for a cop's sick leave, so he could go to the cabin. It would be a place for rest, exercise, and solitary contemplation about what to do with the rest of his life.

Solitary, for his parents were long ago buried in a grassy Milwaukee graveyard. He barely remembered them. His uncle had raised him, taught him, put him in schools when it was convenient, and took him on expeditions all over the world. Roland Targo's name was familiar to many people who couldn't quite remember if he was a Mafia godfather or an ethnic chef on PBS. A few had read his magazine articles, such as "Blood Brother to the Headhunters" or "With Our Living Ancestors" in popular magazines. College students still used his books for supplementary reading in anthropology courses.

Jason saw a sign stretched across the highway. Lake Mills was just ahead. Would the old Aztlan Mounds State Park be the same? On an impulse, he turned off, drove through the small town, and on to the mounds. He parked the car and walked to the top of the largest one, flat-topped, square, and terraced. It seemed as he remembered it. So was the reconstructed log palisade. Similar high, chinked logs had once protected the Indian village until its neighbors burned the walls and slaughtered everyone who lived there.

When had he been here with Roland? Fifteen years before? That was almost half a lifetime ago.

His uncle was ancient then. Of course, when you're a teenager, anyone even middle-aged is—what was Unk's favorite word for it? Antediluvian. Roland must have been in his middle sixties when they visited Aztlan.

He used to say his opinions were neither young nor old, just practical. Actually, if you pinned him down, he would admit his ideas were as old as the Cro-Magnons, because people hadn't changed much, except to have bigger tools and smaller brow ridges. Jason remembered what Roland had said, so long ago, when he pointed to the park sign. "It says the people who lived here were cannibals. Some anthropologists think the Cro-Magnons killed off the Neanderthals and then ate them. Maybe so. We don't know for sure. Nobody left any diaries. But some of the human bones found in the big barbecue pit here were split the long way, as if somebody tried to get out the marrow to eat it. We're still cannibals, even if we don't literally have each other for dinner these days. Seems like there's always somebody snappin' at your ass. Life is like the food pyramid. There's plenty of room at the bottom, but you don't get to the top unless somebody else falls off or gets eaten by the cannibals."

Jason walked between the mounds, his hands in his pockets. He felt the slight breeze ruffle his yellow crew cut, and smelled the freshly mowed grass under his feet.

It probably covered the remains of the people of Aztlan, who wouldn't recognize the name. The Indians here had never been Aztecs. The first Whites just assumed the mounds had been built by the Aztecs, the Indians who tore the hearts from their human sacrifices.

Roland had pointed to the largest mound and said, "That's probably where they had the sacrifices and ate the victims." Then he had shrugged and added, "Or maybe not."

His practical opinions were sometimes somewhat strange.

He would say astrology was bullshit. He also said he was a

Libra, and all Libras believed astrology was bullshit.

Roland had strong opinions about Jason's future. "Be a carpenter," Roland had said, "or a teacher. Teaching is like carpentry. You pound ideas like nails into people's heads to construct knowledge.

"Don't be a cop. A cop's job puts him in the middle of the cannibals.

"Don't be a preacher, either. A preacher spouts junk nobody believes. People don't believe in the hereafter. If they believed in hell, they'd be afraid to sin, and we wouldn't need preachers.

"Some people do believe in the supernatural, but maybe that's just stuff we don't understand. If we understood it, it'd be natural. And if the supernatural is natural stuff we don't understand, there's plenty of that around. We don't know why the sky is blue or what makes aspirin work."

As Jason drove back to the highway, he remembered Roland had once said, "There's enough supernatural stuff up at the cabin on Windigo Pond to scare the hell out of anybody, if somebody goes looking for it."

Jason didn't intend to look for it. He'd be satisfied with the natural when he got there.

The Honda rolled smoothly through small towns that could have been designed by Norman Rockwell. Downtowns still had brick buildings topped with cement pediments. Square, grassy parks where Civil War cannons guarded stone, crenellated courthouses. In the countryside, Jason drove past white, two-story, clapboard, pitched-roof farmhouses with pillared front porches. Sometimes an American flag drooped from a pole in the front yard. He almost expected to see the American Gothics standing in front, Mr. Gothic firmly gripping his pitchfork, with his dour, disapproving wife beside him.

10

The towns had typical Middle American names: Friendship, Bakerville, and Colby, where a small sign proclaimed the town as the home of Colby cheese.

He knew it wasn't all a Rockwell landscape. Behind a white farmhouse, a leaning, rickety barn stuffed with moldy hay might slowly rot in the summer rains and winter blizzards. It could be a symbol of the hidden evil (he almost laughed at the thought) that lurks in the hearts of men.

Not far away, the inspiration for Norman Bates had lived, a psycho too macabre for even Hitchcock to portray truthfully. Ed Gein had killed women, flayed their bodies, and worn their skins while he pranced around in his shabby, lonely shack.

Jason would be driving on to Jackpine, near Windigo Pond. The town should be peaceful even now, in August, when it bulged with thousands of fishermen from all over the country.

Jason couldn't remember real crime in Jackpine. Drunk drivers occasionally hit a tree or a deer. Most excitement came from petty thefts or bar fights. Names of people with overdue videotapes were disclosed in the weekly newspaper. Sometimes the most violent crimes were breaking and entering, committed at a lake cabin by a hungry bear.

Late in the afternoon, he drove into the deep, dank, darkly green Jackpine National Forest. A thin beam of afternoon sun lit the gap where the road cut between the tall trees. Jason would soon be at the peaceful cabin. He was pretty sure it would be there, as serene and unspoiled as before.

Except, he reminded himself, Uncle Roland was missing.

Chapter 2

Fearsome Critters

Jason stopped at the corner of Peavey and Sawmill, at the only traffic light in Jackpine. Ever since he could remember, this was "The Crossroads." One highway went south to Madison and north to the ore boat docks at Ashland. On the east-west highway, the closest big cities were in Minnesota and Michigan.

The old library hadn't changed. The two-story stone building still had the cement pillars that seemed to identify every Carnegie Library he'd ever seen. For Jackpine, the building was middling new. Some buildings dated from the middle 1870s, when the first timber cruisers saw the potential wealth of the great pine forests of this part of Northern Wisconsin.

He drove past each old building with the pleasant sense of familiarity, like greeting old friends.

Of course, things had changed since the days when lumberjacks stamped their calked boots up and down Peavey Street from the sawmill (on Sawmill Street, of course) to the nearby whorehouses and saloons along the Jackpine River on Water Street.

Some things had changed since he was a kid, spending time here with Unk Roland. Other things never seemed to change. Even the tourists looked the same. Traffic stalled as people crowded the sidewalk and ambled into the street. They licked ice cream cones, showed each other their souvenir T-shirts with pictures of loons or muskies. Some wore "Bear Whiz Beer" shirts, showing a bear peeing into a woodland stream. Some of the hats proudly proclaimed they were worn by an "Old Fart" or even an "Old Fart's Wife."

Jason didn't have to count the streets, for they were named First, Second, and on to the last one, Sixth, on the edge of the Pine Tree Country Club and Golf Course.

He drove past the town park, named for a half-forgotten lumber baron who'd donated the land. He turned left, drove two blocks, and found the low, brick building. He didn't need to see the sign on the wall. He couldn't miss the green and white sheriff's department cars parked in front.

Inside, it was almost dim, with light filtered through Venetian blinds. He heard only a fan's quiet hum, and felt the breeze push some cool air out the door. This place seemed more like an office than a police area, although he smelled the usual cigarette smoke. Then he realized the difference between this and a big city police station. He didn't smell marijuana, mildew, B.O., vomit, and urine.

In the corner, a man in a khaki uniform sat behind a battered wooden desk. His uniform seemed to blend into the greenish walls behind him. He didn't rise, just nodded and asked, "Help you?"

Jason also nodded as he walked forward. "I'd like to see the sheriff. Skinner, isn't it?"

"That's right, but he isn't in. Might be here soon. Anything I can help you with?"

"I'm Jason Targo, Roland Targo's nephew."

As he approached, he realized the deputy was Indian, probably a Buckskin, lean, his face a light coffee color.

"Ahmeek," said the deputy, smiling.

Jason had almost forgotten that name. He grinned. Ahmeek was king of the beavers. Because of Roland's stubby nose and large upper front teeth with a gap between the incisors, the nickname naturally fit. No, not a nickname, Jason corrected himself, but an Indian name. Charley Rogers gave it to Roland when he was adopted into the tribe.

The deputy rose and stuck out a hand. "Jack Mink. Glad to meet you. I didn't know your uncle. I met him once, saw him in town and on the reservation a few times. I'm sorry he's missing. Have a seat."

Jason realized Mink was in his mid-thirties. If they had played together as children, they obviously didn't remember each other. Maybe Mink had lived on a different part of the reservation or even in a boarding school. Jason looked around, picked up a sturdy captain's chair that could have been in one of the local taverns, pulled it to the front of the desk, and sat. "What can you tell me about what happened?"

Mink shrugged. "Not much. I think the sheriff called you once or twice, didn't he?"

Jason nodded.

"He probably told you all we knew," the deputy continued. "We got a call from the tribal police. Old Charley Rogers had gone by the cabin, and the professor wasn't there. I mean, Doctor Targo. Hell, we all knew him as Roland, or Ahmeek or, well, you know how kids are, they sometimes called him old man beaver face. I don't really know what his right title was."

Jason shrugged. "Doesn't make much difference now, does it?"

Mink shook his head. "The tribal police searched the area and then called us. Sheriff Skinner and I went out and looked around. It's private land, of course, even if it's almost sur-

14

rounded by the reservation, so it's in our jurisdiction."

Jason noticed a slight lightening in the room and looked around. The front door had opened silently as a man entered, trailing smoke from the cigar in his mouth. He was bulky, with a bald head surrounded by a horseshoe of white wispy hair. He tossed his Stetson (khaki colored, like the rest of his uniform) toward a mounted elk head on a wall. The hat barely caught on the tip of an antler.

Mink said, "Sheriff, this is Jason Targo, Roland's nephew."

Skinner advanced, holding out a hand. "Glad to meet you, Mr. Targo. No, dammit, I'm sorry we have to meet. It's the circumstances, you know. I guess you must be Roland's only living relative."

Jason nodded.

"He's been asking about the professor," said Mink. "I told him about Charley finding the cabin empty, and us searching."

"We looked as much as we could," said Skinner. "There'd been a heavy snow. If he was buried in it, there was no way to find him. I mean, we poked at lumps, but we only found logs, fallen branches, stuff like that. We saw some animal tracks, but no human ones except for Charley's, so we couldn't tell which way your uncle went. Of course, we've had our eyes open since the snow melted. The Indians have too, but nobody's reported finding his . . ." he paused, "him."

He sat on the edge of the desk, puffed the cigar for a moment, then said, "You know much about these woods?"

Mink told Skinner, "He lived here when he was a kid, with Roland. Even if we didn't know him, we knew about him."

"Then maybe you know what could happen in the woods," said Skinner. "He could have had a heart attack while he was chopping wood. Maybe he went fishing on the

15

lake and fell through the ice. Could have shot himself accidentally, or been shot by some hunter. Happens all the time
here. People even get killed by deer sometimes. People die,
they might never be found, and nobody ever finds out what
happened to them. Maybe you've heard about the strange animals that used to roam around these North Woods. Old Paul
Bunyan stories about the hodag, hoop snake, hidebehind,
things like that. 'Fearsome critters,' they were called. Those
were just tall tales, but there's some nasty real animals. Bear,
coyotes, big cats. Wolves, too. Not many, but a few have been
seen near here."

He puffed again, thought, and added, "Now I remember.
You're a police officer, aren't you?"

"Milwaukee," said Jason.

"I remember you asked a bunch of questions when I talked
to you on the phone. But you didn't come up here."

"I was in the hospital."

"Nothing serious, I hope," said Skinner, with what
seemed to be false politeness, as though implying that a little
trip to the hospital shouldn't have kept Jason from coming to
help look for his uncle.

"Enough to keep me there for a few months," said Jason.

"Ah," said the sheriff, softly. "You seem to have recov-
ered, though."

"I've still got nerve damage in the back. I was paralyzed for
a while. Might still be again, if it gets aggravated.

"I'm on sick leave."

"Car accident?" asked Mink.

"Bullet. Some trouble with a dope dealer."

"Well, you probably wouldn't have been able to help
much if you'd been up here," said Skinner. He frowned and
studied his cigar. "We don't know why he was at the cabin in
the middle of winter. You know why?"

16

"Like I said when you called then, I don't know."

"Rough place to be in the winter," said Mink, "especially for an old man."

"He was in good shape for his age," said Jason.

"Still, he wasn't young. You don't think he was hunting?"

"No. He used to hunt, but not much with a rifle."

"Bow hunter?"

Jason smiled. "In South America, when we lived with the Caribs, he used to bring down birds with blow gun darts tipped with curare. With the Eskimos, he harpooned seals. He and I lived with various tribes while he did his anthropological studies. The FirstMen weren't the only people who adopted him."

Mink nodded thoughtfully at Jason's use of the Buckskins' own name for themselves.

"Anyway, he probably wasn't in good enough shape to be dragging a dead deer through the woods," muttered Skinner, "so I'd assume he wasn't hunting."

Mink said, "He didn't spend all his time at the cabin. I know he visited his old friends on the reservation and in town. It must have been pretty lonely out there in the winter. With the roads all snowed in, there was hardly any way to get around. I guess he traveled mostly by snowmobile. We found one beside his pickup."

Skinner walked through a door behind Mink's desk and gestured for Jason to follow.

The next room was pine paneled and decorated with pictures, diplomas and news clippings. Jason didn't have a chance to study them, for Skinner went to a cluttered desk, opened the top drawer, and fished around in it. He finally picked out some tagged keys.

"Here's the keys to his truck. It's still parked there. The batteries are probably dead by now, but you got a jumper cable, you can start it up if you need to. Here's the key for the front door. We put a hasp and lock on it. Wouldn't keep anybody out who really wanted to get in, but it's the best we could do. I can't guarantee the place hasn't been robbed or vandalized."

Mink, as he entered, said, "Nobody would come there from the reservation side of the lake, anyway. With Roland gone and, you know, you have to face it, probably dead, the cabin's like a cursed place. None of the Buckskins would touch it."

Skinner said, "I don't know about the tourists. They've been on the lake for months. Even the local people, some of them might have gone in there and taken stuff."

He paused, then turned to Mink. "I know how most of your people respect things like the professor and his cabin, but I think there are a few who don't."

He turned back to Jason. "How did he get along with the Buckskins? Did he have trouble with any of them?"

"Not that I heard," said Jason. "He was an honorary member of the tribe, but you already know that."

Skinner frowned and puffed. "He ever study them? Write about them?"

"No," said Mink. He looked at Jason. "Isn't that right?"

"He was just a friend, a neighbor. Besides, there'd been other studies of the Buckskins."

Skinner shrugged. "Well, there's been some trouble now and then. Mostly from the young men. They're getting," and he grinned at Mink, "what shall I call them, Jack? Uppity?"

"Militant," said Mink, grinning back. "Or hard-assed, ornery, greedy, depending on whom you're talking to. We have problems. Too much booze, too little work. Culture conflicts, even among our own people. A few of them, mostly the younger ones, like the sheriff says, they aren't so much militant as they are just plain mean. It's the same on every reservation. And not just with Indians. It's the same in every city and town in the country these days."

Skinner said, "Some of them have been talking about getting the land back."

"Like dancing back the buffalo?" asked Jason.

Skinner seemed puzzled. "What's that? A buffalo dance?"

"The Ghost Dance," said Jason. "The Sioux wanted to bring back the buffalo. That was when there were just a few of them left. So the medicine men painted some shirts and said they had enough magic to stop bullets. It didn't work, of course. Next came the Battle of Wounded Knee. Well, maybe that was closer to a massacre. A few soldiers were killed, but they might have shot each other. More than two hundred Sioux were killed."

"Buckskins aren't doing any magic or dancing," said Skinner. "Are they, Jack?"

The deputy shook his head. "Mostly it's been talk, sometimes some picketing. Nobody's done anything violent."

"Unless somebody did it to Roland," Skinner added. "There's been some arguments with, what's his name, Jack? Guy thinks he's the leader."

"Whitefish, Bobby Whitefish. Used to be Bobby Dixon. He's been talking about organizing pickets to protest the tourists fishing in Indian water."

"Bobby Dixon?" said Jason. "We played together when we were kids. We were good friends, but we haven't been in touch for so many years that I don't know what he'd be like now."

"Things change," said Skinner. "Your childhood friends aren't just playing these days. If your uncle got crosswise with some of them, well, let's say there's other kinds of fearsome critters out there."

19

Chapter 3

The Ice Skeleton

After the cool quiet of the sheriff's office, the streets seemed more hot, sweaty and bustling than before. At the IGA store, Jason bought the few things he'd need at the lake, mostly food, and a red can of gas for the generator.

He drove west on the highway, between gently sloping pastures and fields of foot-high corn. He passed more Rockwell farmhouses, often with grape arbors in the front yards. Ahead, he saw a scummy green pond lined with cattails, and then a sign pointing south with an arrow and "Buckskin Indian Reservation" on it. He turned at the sign and drove south, entering the forest, greenly shadowed under a late afternoon sun. He didn't need a sign to tell him he'd entered the reservation. The asphalt ended and the road became rutted and narrow. A sign alongside the road told him, "Buckskin, 9 Mi."

He drove about two miles, slowly, looking for the turnoff.

There it was, almost hidden in pine branches. The mailbox, with the simple, hand-lettered, "Targo" had been tipped over by a vandal, car, or perhaps even a frightened deer. He turned left and drove on the winding road between trees that gently brushed the side of the car. After almost two miles, the road topped a slight hill. Jason stopped the car for a few minutes while he looked down on the cabin. It was as he remembered it, from last year and all the way back to when he was a kid running through the trees with Bobby Dixon and his other Buckskin friends.

The small, one-room frame cabin was covered with pine slabs, throwaways from the lumber mill, so it looked like Abe Lincoln's birthplace. The green asphalt roofing seemed to be all there. The stovepipe chimney still tilted a bit, but it hadn't fallen yet. The front door was closed and the windows he could see weren't broken.

Beyond the cabin, he saw dark, tree-framed Windigo Pond.

He slowly drove down into the shallow basin and parked next to the pickup beside the house. Someone had put the snowmobile into the pickup bed. They seemed to be all right.

Skinner's key opened the padlock on the door, and Jason entered. With the curtains drawn, the interior had a spectral dimness. He crossed the room and pulled back the curtains on the windows facing the lake.

The lake was always the same: dark, brooding in the late afternoon gloom. It seemed almost haunted, as Roland had sometimes hinted it was.

As his eyes adjusted to the dimness, he could see the flickering glows of fires on the shaded campsites on the other side of the lake. On the north, his left, the few other privately owned cabins or resorts hid behind a peninsula that jutted across water as smooth and flat as a black plate.

Windigo Pond was part of South Creek, which flowed from Jackpine Lake, to the north, southward to empty into the Wisconsin River. The pond's half-mile diameter could have qualified it for a lake, but there was already a Windigo Lake to the east, near the resort town of Hayward. Local people, at least those with a dark sense of humor, sometimes acknowledged the pond's original Indian name by calling it "Cannibal Lake."

Jason felt alone in the wilderness, but then he heard a hum that soon became a putting roar. Somewhere on the lake was a motorboat, probably leaving a trail of empty beer cans in its white V of a wake.

Jason grinned as he looked around. Wilderness, well, Walden, it ain't.

And yet, he remembered, Thoreau's cabin on Walden Pond was closer to Concord than Roland's cabin was to Jackpine. Thoreau visited neighbors and had visitors himself. He walked to town almost every day so he could read the newspaper. Even so, Thoreau found a microcosm of the world in his yard when he watched a deadly battle between red and black ants, and saw a mink stealthily murder a frog.

Years ago, Jason had decided that all the world was a wilderness, and humanity was wildlife. Then he remembered that Uncle Roland was missing.

The cabin's lights and icebox ran off a generator, but he decided to postpone trying to start it. Instead, he found the gas lantern, filled it, pumped it, and lit it. The harsh white light brightened the room enough for him to see what Roland had left.

The rumpled and unmade spindle bed may have been an antique when Roland bought it at a junk shop thirty or so years ago. On the other side of the room, the cot where Jason had slept many times was folded and leaned against the wall. The south wall had a small sink and, above it, a cast iron hand pump. The water had two temperatures, cold and colder, depending on how much you pumped. He tried it and got nothing but a creaky wheeze. A trip to the lake for priming water would cure that.

He opened the door of the pot-bellied heating stove in the

middle of the cabin and saw half-burned pieces of wood.

He stared cautiously at the refrigerator, wondering what might ooze out if he opened it. He finally did. It was warm, of course, and smelled slightly stale, but he found, to his relief, that it was bare. Someone, possibly Charley Rogers, had cleaned it out before the cabin was locked.

The room had a musty odor, but nothing sinister, only the smell one would expect in a room closed for months. He went back to the door and opened it. When he opened the lakeside door, he felt a slight breeze move through the cabin.

Roland's old portable typewriter squatted on the small desk in front of a window that faced the lake. The few sheets of typing paper on the desk had not been used. The shallow drawer held only a few pencil stubs, a ball point pen, and an eraser. The wastebasket beside the desk had only a spider web inside.

Judging from the blank paper, Roland hadn't been working on anything. A few paperback mysteries were stacked on the small shelf above the typewriter and, what seemed somewhat surprising, an old paperback copy of Eric Hoffer's book about fanaticism, *The True Believer*.

Jason stood in the center of the room and slowly turned, studying the interior of the cabin. When he looked behind the few pictures on the walls, he found only more sparse cobwebs. He flipped back the blankets and looked under the mattress. Nothing unusual there.

The cabin was just as he would expect it. Roland's research books weren't there, for they would be in his office at the university library at Madison.

Jason walked down to the edge of the lake, sat on a stump, and looked out at the darkening water. A few lanterns lit boats in the middle of the lake.

As he turned to go back to the cabin, he saw a piece of 1x8

pine board nailed to a tree that faced the lake. The message painted on it was, "No Trespassing. By Order of the Buckskin Indian Tribe." An arrow stuck in the sign like an exclamation point. Not a light target arrow, he noticed, but a heavy hunting shaft with a broad steel tip half buried in the wood. Whoever put it there had used a powerful bow.

However, the land and cabin belonged to Roland, not the tribe. Perhaps one of Roland's Indian friends had put the sign there. If the arrow was meant to be a stronger warning against vandals, it had worked.

Walking up the slight slope to the cabin, he felt his feet beginning to drag, and he slumped in sudden exhaustion. Too much time in the hospital, not enough exercise, and the drive from Milwaukee all caught up with him at that moment.

And, to make things worse, he sensed a numbness in his back. He wondered if it was going to act up again. He didn't need that.

Moving carefully, he unfolded the cot, unrolled the thin mattress, then went to the car to get his sleeping bag. He spread it on top of the mattress and sat on it.

Beer would be good, he decided. The six pack of Leinenkuegels in the car was still cold, so he pulled one off, popped the top, and took a deep, satisfying drink. Several more long swallows finished off the can. He belched and tossed the empty toward the wastebasket. It hit the wall and bounced to the floor. No two points, but what the hell, he was batching it. He'd pick it up in the morning. He turned off the lantern, lay down on top of the sleeping bag, and tried to remember what he'd seen here, the thing out of place.

A spot of white in the room's darkness caught his eye. He remembered something in a Sherlock Holmes story about the dog that didn't bark, but should have. If there were no envelopes or stamps in the desk drawer, why was the paper beside the typewriter? If Roland wasn't writing a letter, he may have been working on something else. Someone might have taken his research, notes and any typed pages. Jason made a mental note to ask Skinner or Mink if any papers or other books had been found when the place was searched. He had to assume that it had been searched by someone.

He stretched out flat, knowing sleep would come soon. It was something he both needed and dreaded. It came almost as soon as he closed his eyes, but later, some time in the middle of the night, his unconscious mind told him, "Wake up. Here comes that damned dream again."

It always started the same way. Slick, shiny ice-coated Milwaukee's winter streets. The squad car, parked kitty-corner, blocked the intersection. Jason's partner stood behind him, gun drawn, held in both hands, aimed down the street. His targets were two people with faces hidden in the shadows of their parkas. Jason couldn't make out their features, their sexes, or even their races. But, somehow, he knew they were bearded males. Their eyes glittered in the glow of the traffic lights. The men pointed guns at Jason and his partner. Which partner? There had been several over the years, and Jason couldn't guess which one was behind him. Nonsense. He knew which one, of course; he just couldn't remember his name or what he looked like.

The noise behind him sounded like a firecracker's pop, not at all like the explosion of a .38 Police Special.

He started to run. He knew that was wrong. He hadn't run when it really happened. But in the dream, he ran down Layton Avenue toward the airport. Maybe he hoped to get on a plane and fly to safety. But he knew he couldn't. In every dream since he woke up in the hospital, he never ran faster than the bullet that chased him. It was large as a cannon ball, zigzagging back and forth as if in an old pinball machine. It caromed off a lamp post, ricocheted off the hood of a car, and skimmed a puddle of ice. It always bounded closer and closer. In a few seconds, it would catch up and he'd feel the dull thud in his back.

He almost sobbed with relief. He knew he would fall forward and then would sit upright in the bed, gasping, holding a hand to his back. When he took his hand away, it would be smeared with blood. When he discovered only sweat, the dream would be finished and he really would be awake.

But this dream was different. Before the bullet hit him, he turned to watch it bounding toward him. This time he'd face it so it couldn't hit him in the back.

But instead of a bullet, a skeleton pursued him. The rack of bones was taller than the pine trees it ran between.

Pine trees? On Layton Avenue?

He was on frozen Windigo Pond as he tried to run from the skeleton. It wasn't made of bones, but of ice. Its icicle fingers clutched the air as it approached. Deep inside the ribs, it had a pulsating heart of ice.

He knew what it was. He knew its name. But, like the name of his partner, he just couldn't remember.

He turned and ran faster, but his feet slid on the ice. He felt like the Roadrunner, with his feet going around in the air, waiting for the Coyote to catch up with him. But when he did, Jason wouldn't fly ahead in the air. Coyote would catch him and tear him to pieces.

He sat upright, as he always did, gasping, and put his right hand to his back.

Sure enough, it was wet. He stared at the bloody smear on his palm. He held out his hand, into the moonlight that streamed through the window. The room lit up from a harsh, bright light, as if someone had set off a flash bulb. Lightning, he realized, and almost immediately heard the rumble of

26

thunder. Not too far away. It seemed like only a second before the flash and the noise. In that brief flash, he had seen that his hand wasn't bloody after all. The dream may have ended differently, but his palm was smeared with the usual sweat. He eased himself carefully back to the cot and waited for the sleep that always came after his heart stopped its own thunder.

The image of the ice skeleton faded from his mind as if lost in a snowstorm, but he knew that somewhere, some time in the past, he had encountered it before.

Nonsense, he thought, drifting into the hazy confusion that preceded sleep. With the crazy logic of someone still half asleep, he realized that it wasn't my dream. It must have been someone else's nightmare.

Chapter 4

Summer People

When the morning sun streamed through the east window, Jason woke and looked at his watch. It was about six o'clock. He could go back to sleep. As he closed his eyes, sputtering motorboats and the muffled voices of early fishermen on the lake canceled that idea. Although he didn't remember it, he had removed his pants and shirt some time during the night. He took off his sweat-sticky underwear, then rummaged through his suitcase for swim trunks and put them on.

The lake wasn't as cold as he expected, but it woke him completely. He floated for a few minutes, letting the water ease his back, then breast stroked back and forth a half dozen times. He swam as far as the edges of his property, for the hundred feet or so had enough space for his exercise. He knew, from childhood experience, swimming too far out into the lake could bring narrow misses from motorboats or water skiers.

The closest fishermen watched him carefully. He thought they might be looking at the sign. Maybe they thought he didn't belong here. They might think he was an Indian. Hell, most of those people came from big cities. They might not know an Indian from a Chinaman unless he had feathers in his hair.

He wondered if he should take down the sign. As Roland's only heir, he owned, or would own, the land and cabin. But whoever put up the sign could take it down. In the meantime, it might still keep people away.

He swam closer to the cabin, let his feet down cautiously, felt for the bottom, and found none. The dropoff was closer to the shore. When he was a kid, he could wade out to his chest before he got to the drop-off. He grinned. In those days, his chest was a lot closer to the ground. He swam a few yards farther and tried again. This time he stood when his feet touched bottom. He took a careful step backwards, then another. On the third step, he felt only water below his foot. This was the edge of the cliff above the river before it was flooded by the downstream dam more than seventy years ago to make the lake.

Somewhere at the bottom was the old Indian village of Buckskin. It had been a permanent town, not of tepees or bark lodges, but of meeting houses and homes of pine boards.

He decided that nothing was permanent, except that the town might be permanently under the lake. He wondered if Indians were still buried there.

He waded out of the water. At the cabin door, he turned and looked back at the lake. Rippling reflections of the sun almost blinded him and silhouetted the boats. Someone in the nearest boat waved. Jason returned it, then entered the cabin.

The weather was too hot to use a towel. Besides, the lake water, clear, cool, and gently flowing, seemed so clean he didn't feel the need to wipe it off.

The exercise had eased his back. He felt more energetic than he had to be. But he was in a lazy mood. He didn't even have to catch a fish for breakfast.

The box of food was still on the kitchen counter, so no animals had helped themselves to breakfast. Maybe the sign even scared off raccoons.

He pumped the Coleman camp stove, wiped dust from a frying pan, and was about to put eggs into it when he remembered the generator behind the cabin. He checked it and, sure enough, the gas had evaporated from the tank. He pulled the gas can from the back seat of the car and filled the tank. After jerking the rope several times, he heard the putt-putting as the generator started pouring electricity into the cabin.

Only the beers needed cooling, so he put them into the icebox. He fried three eggs with a small can of corned beef on the side and washed them down with cold water.

The stack of paper beside the typewriter caught his eye again. If Roland had been working on something, there might be some trace of it.

He took each book from the shelf and quickly flipped through the pages. Inside Hoffer's book, he found a small, folded brochure, something you'd expect to be thrust at you by some shaved-headed robe-wearer at an airport.

"WILDERNESS OF ZIN," it said at the top and, underneath, in bold letters, "And the Tribe of Judah went into the Wilderness of Zin, and they partook of the milk and honey, and of the manna which were the fruit thereof." He assumed that the quote came from the Bible.

Under it was a picture of robed men and women sitting around a campfire. He wondered, roasting something? Weenies, marshmallows, babies? He didn't know why that thought came to mind, except one bearded man looked somewhat wild-eyed, like Thomas Hart Benton's painting of John Brown. Roland probably used the brochure for a bookmark. He usually ignored this sort of propaganda.

As an anthropologist, he'd been familiar with the great variety of worship of gods, demons, planets, rivers, mountains, masks, sticks, stones and broken bones, each the only true god, the only answer to life's questions, and the only true salvation to happiness after death. Usually, he'd been polite and careful. He didn't scoff at the beliefs of people who might be offended, even dangerous. He'd stick his hands in his pockets when approached by anyone who handed out printed pitches, even sale ads or campaign fliers.

Jason decided that if there was no information there, he'd go somewhere else to look. And, as long as he knew the generator was working, he could get more stuff to put in the icebox.

He locked up the cabin, using the sheriff's key and padlock, and reminded himself to buy replacements or find out if Skinner wanted the things returned.

The road through the woods didn't seem as rutted and bumpy as before. Maybe he was getting used to it. Pretty quick he might know where all the holes were, even in the dark. When he stopped at the reservation road, he wondered if he should turn south and visit Charley Rogers. He would know about the sign. Instead, Jason turned right to go to the Jackpine highway. He needed to talk to Sheriff Skinner again. At the highway, he turned right and drove north, but pushed the brake when something on the right side of the road caught his eye.

The mailbox had the name of George Simpson stenciled on the side. Simpson must have moved in recently, Jason thought, but remembered he hadn't been to the cabin for several years.

He turned right on the highway and soon saw a wooden sign tipped over and lying flat in the deep grass. Something about it seemed familiar. He backed the car, pulled to the shoulder, and got out for a better look. The sign's post was broken at the bottom, as if it had been hit by a car. "WILDERNESS OF ZIN" was neatly lettered in black paint, with an arrow pointing to the right. He guessed it had indicated south, where a narrow road seemed squashed between pine trees. He noticed the sign had several bullet holes. Beside the sign, a new mailbox, simply lettered "WILDERNESS," hadn't been vandalized. As he drove on, he wondered if some local people disliked the cult. Maybe the mailbox was a fresh target waiting to be perforated.

In Jackpine, he parked at the sheriff's office and entered. Mink again sat behind his desk. He gestured to the open door when Jason asked if Skinner was in. The sheriff sat in his captain's chair, with his feet on a pile of papers on his desk. He puffed a cigar and motioned for Jason to sit in the other chair.

Jason said, "Next trip, I'll bring back that hasp and lock, if you want it."

"I'd appreciate it," said Skinner. "You can't believe how cheap the county budget can be, even if the money comes from summer tourists. No hurry, though. A lock isn't a big budget item. And I suppose you wonder who searched the place. I did, with Mink and Charley Rogers. Wasn't any big search, just looking around to see if the prof left any notes or anything. We didn't find any. Didn't take anything, either."

"That's what I thought," said Jason. "I figured if you'd found anything of any use, you would have told me."

Skinner nodded and puffed the cigar. "Well, there's nothing new here since yesterday. Everything all right out there?"

"Yes, as far as I can tell. If Roland had any papers, they must have been gone before you got there."

Skinner spread his hands in resignation. "What can I say? If somebody took some stuff, we wouldn't know what it was. All we know is he's gone. If he'd planned to go somewhere, I suppose he'd have told you. So at this point, I also have to assume he's, well, you know."

"Dead," said Jason, nodding. "I'm pretty sure of that.

But I want to find out all I can."

"Naturally," said Skinner, also nodding.

"Does Hester Meldon still run the paper?"

"She does," said Skinner, "but not as much as she used to. Got a sharp girl doing most of the work for her. Name of Erica Chamberlain. Grew up here. Knows everybody."

"I don't remember her," said Jason.

"No reason you should," said Skinner, grinning. "She's local, like I said, and you were one of the summer people."

Jason almost shuddered as he remembered the Shirley Jackson story about the couple who stayed isolated at their summer cabin after the end of the tourist season. They expected to get their food delivered as usual, but the locals let them starve. Was it like that in Jackpine? Was there hidden resentment against the interlopers who invaded the town every year?

"She's real friendly, though," said Skinner. "Even talks to tourists. Don't know why. I don't think they ever read the paper. But then, I don't see much of them folks myself, except when they come in here to bitch about something or get picked up for drunk driving." He grinned again. "Why, some of them might be real people."

"Makes me feel almost human," said Jason. "I'll get the lock back to you. Then you can save some money and buy oats for old Dobbin, the only horse in town."

"Much obliged," said Skinner, with a Santa's twinkle in his eyes.

As Jason left the building, he felt the humidity envelop him like a fog. He thought there was no sense in trying to drive. He'd never find a parking space downtown. By the sheriff's office, two blocks away from Peavey Street, a few people strolled the narrow cement sidewalks. No one seemed in a hurry, not even the lean dog who lagged behind on a leash and looked for a shady patch of grass.

When Jason reached Peavey Street, it was as if he had stepped into a human zoo. Tourists of all ages and sizes crowded the sidewalk. No, maybe not a zoo, Jason decided. It's more like a carnival, but without the garish lights and raucous atmosphere you could find in Times Square, Division Street in Chicago, or even the Wisconsin Dells. As he entered the flow and strolled south, he dodged children with squirt guns or families gawking at window displays, then snaked through a crowd of people listening to a Dixieland band. He crossed in the middle of the street and entered the two-story brick building beside the library.

The sign in the window, "Jackpine News," was hand-lettered on typing paper and stuck on the window with masking tape. As he opened the door, a small bell tinkled, and he felt as if he had left the carnival and entered the 19th century. He peered through floating dust motes to see a desk, where a woman sat in front of a set of shelves piled with stacks of newspapers. The short woman, stern-looking, hair pulled back in a bun, seemed equally old-fashioned. He almost expected her to be speaking into the horn of a crank telephone, but she held a cordless phone in one hand while she fingered the keyboard of a computer with the other.

As Jason entered, she waved at him, said "Customer, call you later," hung up and showed a surprisingly bright and friendly smile. She asked, "Help you?"

"I'd like to get some back copies of the paper."

"How far back?"

"About the first of the year."

She nodded. "No problem. We got 'em. Seventy-five cents a copy. Thinking of buying here? Something like a summer cottage?"

"Why do you think that?" he asked as she turned and

started to pull newspapers off the shelves.

She shrugged. "Just a guess. I don't think you're from around here. Maybe you want some lakefront property. Where you thinking of buying?"

"I'm not. I already have a place."

She turned and put a thick pile of newspapers on the desk. "Oh? Whereabouts?"

"Windigo Pond."

"Windigo Pond, huh? I hadn't heard of anybody buying there."

"It's in the family," said Jason. "We've had it for years."

"You're lucky! It's hard to find good property on Windigo. So much of it's on Indian land, you know, or national forest. And if you got it years ago, it was cheaper."

Jason couldn't help smiling. "Much cheaper. My uncle got it from the Indians for free."

She turned and stared at him. "Are you Jason Targo?"

He nodded and wished he'd kept his mouth shut. He might have invited more questions than he wanted to answer.

"Erica would like to talk to you," she said. "The editor."

"Ah yes. I heard she took over from Hester."

"Sort of. Erica's assistant editor, but she does most of the writing and everything."

From what Jason remembered of Hester Meldon, it was surprising she hadn't retired years ago. But maybe not. The instant she retired and quit poking her nose into the town's news, she might wither and crumble like a dried flower. She wasn't nosy in a gossipy way, but knew everything about everybody, including how much she could publish without aggravating anyone. He reminded himself that it would be a good idea to talk to her. She probably still collected unprintable news.

The woman put the papers on the desk. "That's twenty-four papers. Comes to eighteen dollars, no tax."

As he paid her, she screeched, in a voice loud enough to peel wallpaper, "Erica!" then turned around and ignored him as she put the money into a cash register. Jason felt dismissed, as if he were, after all, not worth bothering with.

Just one of the summer people.

Chapter 5

You Might Have Trouble

Jason heard a muffled voice from the other room. "Blanche? What the hell's going on?"

A small woman entered. She wore jeans and a T-shirt with a picture of a black-and-white, red-eyed loon. One of her breasts pushed out the bird's head; the other emphasized a yellow sun above the body. Jason guessed her age as the late twenties. Her light hair flowed naturally to her shoulders and she reminded him of someone. She reminded him of Janet Leigh in *Psycho*, before she was murdered. She stopped and looked around the office. "Are we being robbed or something?"

"Here's the man you wanted to see," said Blanche in her normal tone. "Jason Targo."

Erica looked at Jason as if he came from outer space, then smiled. "Ah! Yes! Mr. Targo! I would like to talk to you. Got a minute?"

"Plenty of time."

"I'm Erica Chamberlain," she said. When they shook hands, her grip was dry and firm, but not aggressive. She gestured for him to follow, turned, and walked toward the back. Jason followed her faint trail of perfume into a room cluttered with equipment, including an old flat bed press large enough to publish a page of the paper. It was clean and oiled, but had no rollers.

"The original press," she said. "A genuine Chandler and Price Craftsman model. We even have the fonts of cold type, but I don't know if anybody in town could use it, except maybe Hester. Now everything's done by computer. We're all up to date here in Hicksville."

He grinned as he watched her sit behind a cluttered desk. "Yeah. I suppose everybody watches TV by candlelight."

"Some of us have electric candles. Have a seat."

"Are you related to Sheriff Skinner?" he asked.

"No. Why? You think everybody in town belongs to the same family? We're not that much inbred, except for," and she waved her hands toward the north and south, "the Jukes and Kallikak families on each side of us."

"You both like to make fun of this town for us furrigners," he said, grinning again.

"Maybe it's because we'd rather do it ourselves. Some of us don't like to be patronized by people who wear Bear Whiz Beer T-shirts."

He settled himself into the captain's chair. "The sheriff has chairs like this, too."

"They must be a hundred years old. They used to be in the old train station, from what I heard, and later were bought by the guy who owned the Shantyboy Saloon. He sold them when he thought they were too old-fashioned."

Jason nodded as he remembered being in the Shantyboy Saloon when he was a kid. It had old guns and mounted fish on the walls and, in the corners, displays of small stuffed animals in human poses. Squirrels in lumberjack costumes played pool. Glass cases held roistering tomcats frozen in time in their top hats and tuxedos, holding motionless canes. On the bar, a thin vertical tube spouted a small perpetual blue gas flame for lighting cigars. Behind the bar, a large painting of a reclining nude had pieces of cloth draped over strategic places. In the days when the Shantyboy was a bucket of blood where the lumberjacks could be Mickey Finned out of their winter wages, the painting was completely uncovered.

"The rest of the chairs are scattered around," she was saying, "probably still being used. Maybe antique dealers got some. And can you tell me anything about what happened to Roland Targo?"

She didn't pause to switch subjects. Jason wondered if this was her version of ambush interrogation.

"I could say 'no comment.' I probably know less than you do."

She shook her head slightly and settled back into the chair. "I'm not asking as a reporter, not unless there's a real story. So far, there's nothing more than that he disappeared. He was your uncle, right?"

Jason nodded.

"And I understand you're his heir, maybe."

He nodded again. "His only heir."

"I wondered about that."

He wondered why she seemed to consider it her business.

She answered the unspoken question. "He was one of our most famous summer residents. Naturally, people were interested in him and his career. So I was surprised when I heard he'd joined the Wilderness of Zin."

"The what?" Then he remembered the pamphlet and the fallen sign. "What's that, some sort of Biblical sect?"

"They call themselves the Judeans, but around here we usually call them Zinners. They like to quote something about milk and honey and manna in the Wilderness of Zin. It sounds like it's from the Bible, but it isn't. I think Hector Lestray made it up just to sound holy. He's their leader.

When I asked him to explain it, he spouted some mystic double-talk about God being in the trees and rocks and water. God in a rock? If I break it, have I killed God or have I made pebble apostles?"

"Animism," said Jason.

She smiled. "That's fancy talk for a cop. Oh, that's right. You were practically raised by Professor Targo. What about the animals?"

"Animism. The belief that every natural object or animal has its own soul."

"Well, whatever, they believe something like that. They live like the Indians used to, raising a few chickens and pigs and growing simple food in small gardens. They hunt, although I haven't heard of any of them being caught poaching. They live in tepees, but they don't hunt with bows and arrows."

"Makes sense," said Jason. "Bowhunting is for sportsmen. Guns are for people who want to eat."

She held up hooked fingers to indicate quotation marks and used a preachy-pompous voice. "A deeply devoted, peaceful religious community." She shrugged, then grinned. "Of course, that's what some of the others were, too, before they drank poison or set themselves on fire." She paused, almost embarrassed. "I'm sorry. I shouldn't be saying that, if your uncle really joined them."

Jason said, "He wasn't the type to believe stuff like that. But, for all I know, he might have been studying them, like when we lived with the Masai. That was when I was about twelve."

"Aren't they in Africa?"

He nodded. "Tough people, too. The warriors lived on cow blood and milk. Oh, yeah, and beer fermented from honey. Part of the initiation into manhood was to kill a lion.

40

One kid grabbed its tail and the others stabbed it with spears and swords. It wasn't just a macho thing, though. They went after the ones that killed cows. When the kids and I played, we carried little leather toy shields and threw spears at pretend lions. I got pretty good at it, but I wasn't expected to really kill one. I wasn't one of the tribe and I was too young. Besides, they weren't my cows."

He thought a second, then added, "You know, you can live with people like that, speak their language, earn their respect, learn their secrets, even become a member of the tribe, a blood brother. But you're not really one of them. When you're done, you go home and they stay there and drink cow blood. What I'm saying, I guess, is my uncle might have been studying that Zin religion, or whatever it is, but he wouldn't believe in it."

She picked up a pencil, rolled it between her fingers, and frowned in thought. "I didn't print anything about Professor Targo joining them," she finally said. "I know we're supposed to be tolerant towards different religions but, well, if word got out about him joining the Judeans, what would happen to his reputation as a scholar?"

"Right down the toilet."

"Exactly," she said. "I didn't know him, but I had too much respect for his reputation to destroy it."

She took a deep breath, sighed, and continued. "The Zinners would probably like to get their hands on his estate, so you may be hearing from them. And, while I'm at it, I think you might have trouble with some of the Indians, too."

"Thanks for the advice. The sheriff already warned me about them."

"You'd better pay attention."

Chapter 6

Naked in the Woods

After leaving the newspaper office, Jason stopped at the IGA again and bought a padlock and groceries, including another six pack of Leinenkuegels, soft drinks, milk, and steaks. He could stay a few days at the cabin without going back to town.

When he got back to the cabin, he saw something on the front door. He drove closer, stopped, and saw it was a note pinned by an arrow. He got out, walked quickly to the door, and read the note. "Get off Indian land."

The arrow, like the one in the sign by the lake, had red feather fletching and a broad-tipped steel hunting point. He ripped off the note and stuck it into his pocket. He guessed it had to be a mistake. His, in a way. He should have visited Charley Rogers or some other tribal elder. He'd do it tomorrow, get it straightened out. Maybe they didn't know he'd returned. No reason they should know. He hadn't talked to any Indians except the deputy, and maybe he didn't live on the reservation.

He unlocked the door and entered. Everything was the same as when he left. He crossed the room, pulled the curtain, and looked out toward the lake. The bright noon sun seemed to drive away threatening thoughts. He set the bags of groceries on the table, then put the cold stuff into the icebox.

He remembered the grill outside, looked out the window, and saw the little circle of rocks covered by the grate. Deadfall littered the ground, and he could use it to burn a steak.

Was he missing something here? He wished he could have been there to search the place when Unk disappeared.

Roland's shirts, pants, and heavy jackets hung on a rack in one corner. Jason searched the pockets and found only a few unimportant things—nasal inhaler, handkerchiefs, spare change. Roland's important papers, including insurance policies, were in a bank deposit box in Milwaukee, so Jason didn't expect to find anything like that here.

He pulled out the desk drawer and looked underneath and behind it. Nothing was taped there. A small chest of drawers held clothing, mostly shirts, socks, and underwear. But, under underwear in the top drawer, he found a single action, six-shot Ruger revolver, .22 caliber, styled like the Colt Peacemaker.

He remembered shooting it when he was a kid. He and Bobby Dixon were bawled out, and he almost got his ass tanned for shooting at tin cans in the lake. He'd been lucky. Unk had told them how even a .22 bullet could go for a half mile and kill somebody.

He had never wondered what had happened to Bobby. But, what the hell, they hadn't met for the last twenty years. They probably wouldn't recognize each other.

The revolver brought back childhood memories, but it was no toy. He hefted it in his hand, surprised at how light the gun was. His hand was too large for it now but, of course, he'd had much smaller hands when he was a kid. Unk Roland had small hands, too. The grip would have been right for him.

Jason flipped out the loading gate and spun the cylinder. It was unloaded. He searched the dresser for bullets, but didn't find any.

He sat at the table, popped the tab on a root beer, and drank deeply. He swatted at mosquitoes as he ate an apple and an orange. They satisfied his lunch hunger, and for the rest of the day he lay on the cot, read a paperback mystery and dozed.

He woke in the sunset's dimness and broiled a steak on the grill. That and a cold beer were enough for supper. He sat on the ground, ate, and watched fishing boats move back and forth in the twilight. He saw an occasional glint of a flashlight or the glimmer of a cigarette lighter. He sometimes heard words muffled by distance. When a cool breeze drifted from the lake, he heard bits of conversation as clearly as if the people stood next to him.

After he saw a flash of lightning across the lake, he heard oars splash into water, and the putting of outboard motors as fishermen headed for the safety of shore. The world seemed suddenly darker in contrast to the lightning, and the somber mood was accentuated by a loon cackling crazily somewhere on the water. Round dimples of rain dotted the water but, fortunately for the boaters, there was no more lightning.

Did something about this lake seem eerie, threatening? There was the name, of course. He remembered the game he'd played with Bobby and the other kids. The one who drew the short straw became the windigo. He put leaves on his head for natural camouflage as he hid in the bushes. The other kids walked in a line, each holding the belt of the one in front. As they approached, the windigo leaped out of the bushes, grabbed someone and pretended to eat him.

Great sport for kids, but Charley Rogers had told them a real windigo had once lived at the lake. That was years ago, about the time the FirstMen fought the Sioux for control of the area.

What a disgusting thought—some primitive wild man creeping through the woods gnawing on somebody's thighbone. Yet, it was just as possible as Jeffrey Dahmer sitting in his stinky Milwaukee apartment and doing the same thing.

It didn't help him sleep later that night.

Somehow, he knew the dream would return.

He decided that was enough of the ice skeleton. It chased him before, and it isn't any fun.

When it appeared, it was as large as a pine tree. Its shiny, silvery skull had a grinning, gap-toothed rictus. The arm bones flapped loosely, reminding him of the dance of the skeletons in *Fantasia*. As he watched, the thing jerked off its skull and threw it. It hit the ice behind him with a solid thunk.

Thunk!

He sat upright in the cot, covered with sweat. If the dream hadn't been real, the sound was. It had been, he realized, a knock on the door.

Then, in the distance, he heard someone shout, "Come on out, White-eye!"

Kids throwing rocks, he guessed. A dawn light streamed into his face. When he got out of bed and looked out an east window, he saw early boats on the sparkling lake. When he looked out a west window, he saw the sun hadn't reached into the woods.

Dim figures blended into the trees. He estimated half a dozen people. They stood in the driveway at the edge of the woods, about a hundred feet from the cabin.

As he opened the door and stepped outside, one cupped a hand around his mouth and shouted, "Get off our land!"

Others began to shout.

"This is Indian land!"

"We are the FirstMen!"

"This land is our land!"

Jason thought he might holler that this land was his land, make it a Woody Guthrie sing-along. But he said nothing, just waited to see what would happen. A few of them waved their arms, as if scaring bears, but didn't come closer.

A tall, thin man with hair tied by a red bandanna stepped forward a few feet.

"You were told to get off," he said.

"I belong here," said Jason, so quietly that some of the men had to lean forward to hear him.

"No," the tall one said. "It belonged to someone else, and he's dead."

"It belonged to my uncle. If he's dead, then it's mine."

The men, suddenly silent, looked at each other, as if in confusion, then the tall one said, "Jason?"

"I'm Jason Targo. Maybe you knew my uncle."

The tall man strode forward, his hand outstretched. "Hey, Jason, I'm Bobby Whitefish. Used to be Dixon. Remember me?"

Jason grinned back and pumped the hand enthusiastically.

"Hell, yes! I remember you, but I haven't seen you for how long, twenty years?"

Bobby nodded. "Something like that. Somebody told me you were a cop and you got killed."

"Half right," said Jason, "and almost right on the other half."

"I'm sorry to hear about the prof," said Bobby.

"He was a fuckin' land-stealin' White-eye," said a man in the crowd.

Bobby turned his head slightly to speak. "Shut up, Willard."

"Don't tell me to—"

Bobby shouted, "Shut up or I'll tear your nose off."

Willard clamped his mouth shut in a tight line and glared at Bobby, then at Jason.

"Willard gets a little hot now and then," said Bobby, calmly. "Maybe he listens to me too much. They say we're kind of militant. Maybe you heard."

"Yeah, I heard something about that. Somebody said you're the leader."

"Maybe, and maybe not. Some of the others, the older ones, were trying to get our land back, but they weren't getting anywhere. So I'm helping them now. I don't call myself a leader. Not a chief or medicine man, nothing like that. And despite what Willard says, I really am sorry about your uncle. We all liked him, and he helped us years ago when we needed it."

"We never needed help from the White-eyes," snarled Willard.

"Yeah, we did, and we got it from him. And we need all the help we can get now, Willard."

Jason thought that this sure as hell wasn't the way to get it.

Willard opened his mouth again and Bobby shouted, "You dumb shit! Shut up!"

Obviously, that kind of talk impressed Willard.

Bobby spoke to Jason again. "We didn't know who you were. And as for it being yours, there might be some legal arguments there. You see, it was given to the prof, so it should revert to us."

"As you said, a legal matter," said Jason. "And, legally, he isn't dead, just missing."

"Missing for good," Willard muttered. "And like you said, Bobby, you ain't our boss. We all got a say, and I say we make this White-eye disappear, just like old beaver face did."

Jason felt a sudden flush of anger color his face, and he felt tempted to step forward and punch the Indian.

47

Apparently sensing Jason's wrath, Willard took his right hand from behind his back and showed a heavy hunting bow. He took a broad-bladed hunting arrow in the same hand and quickly nocked it.

Jason felt naked in the woods without the familiar, comfortable weight of a revolver on his hip.

Bobby shouted, "I told you to shut up, Willard! And put that thing away!"

Willard lowered the bow and arrow to his side, and Jason slowly exhaled a sigh of relief.

If the others noticed, they paid no attention, for their heads slowly turned as they listened to another noise. From behind them, in the road through the trees, came the muffled mutter of a motor. Bobby raised his right hand and made a sweeping motion, left to right. The others seemed to understand it, for they drifted off into the trees and brush. In a few seconds, all but Bobby had disappeared.

"Nice to see you again," he said. "Honest, I thought you were dead and some squatter was here. But you got to remember, Jase, this is FirstMen land. You're welcome to stay a while, but sooner or later you'll have to move out."

He waved once and followed the others into the wood.

Jason took a deep breath and tried to calm himself. His heart slowly stopped hammering in his chest. Whatever had caused it, fear, anger, or both, had disappeared as quickly as Bobby and his friends. The guy, Willard, was probably bragging, showing how tough he was, just like the gang kids in Milwaukee. Still, they killed people sometimes, and it was good Bobby was there.

He heard them crashing through the brush like clumsy bears and couldn't help grinning. They made more noise than he and Bobby had, as kids, when they pretended to ambush a wagon train.

Chapter 7

The Judeans

The truck's noise grew louder as Jason put on socks, jeans, and a light blue, long-sleeved shirt that might slow down the mosquitoes before they sank their noses into his skin. As he put on his shoes, he heard the motor outside in the clearing. He looked out the window to see a green pickup parked outside, rumbling and shuddering.

The driver turned off the motor and climbed out. The tall, thin, bearded man wore an outfit of a light tan shirt and pants. His headband had scraggly feathers stuck in it.

As Jason stepped outside, the man held up a hand and said, "Greetings, brother. May we be welcome here?"

Jason shrugged, watched, and said nothing. The man seemed to take that for a welcome. He turned and motioned to the truck. Two others climbed out of the cab. They also wore tan clothing, headbands, and feathers. One of them, Jason realized, was a woman. She appeared to be in her late twenties, with dark hair down to her shoulders. She smiled at him. With her small nose, it reminded him of a pixie's mischievous grin. However, her full figure was definitely unpixielike. The other man wore a stiff smile that didn't reach his eyes. He was older, Jason guessed, in his forties, smaller and chunkier than the others.

"You must be Jason," said the tall man. "I'm Hector Lestray."

Jason said, "You're the people who live up on the north side of the lake, right?"

Lestray moved forward and stuck out his hand. When they shook, his grip was firm, his fingers sinewy. "Yes. We are the Zinners," he said, grinning. "I know that's what they call us. We call ourselves the Judeans. The New Judeans, actually, a lost tribe of Israel found again in a new Wilderness of Zin."

He withdrew the hand, almost reluctantly, and gestured to the others. "Margaret Stuart and Jim O'Kelly. If we had formal titles, they'd be my assistants."

Still with her pixie smile, Margaret walked forward. When she shook hands, she put her left hand on his right one and patted it. O'Kelly's handshake was brief, tight, and dry. He replaced his smile with a scowl as he stepped back and leaned against the fender of the pickup.

Jason recognized Lestray from the picture of the John Brown look-alike in the brochure. In person, however, he looked less fanatical. He seemed to exude an aura of aesthetic holiness that almost demanded reverence. It was, Jason suddenly realized, probably because he looked like the face on the Shroud of Turin. He guessed that Lestray knew it, too, and had grown the beard to emphasize the resemblance.

"We welcomed your uncle," he said. "Somehow, I feel an auspicious omen in our names. Roland and Hector and Jason, all named after heroes. From the first time I met him, I felt he was destined to become one of us. He did, and I feel that you will too. Your uncle would have become quite important in our movement if he hadn't, well, you understand."

Jason turned his back and walked toward the door. He felt he'd had enough of Lestray and his smooth insinuations. And the others? He heard footsteps on the gravel and turned.

Lestray was right behind him. The others had followed him like smiling shadows.

"I hope there's room in your heart for us, as there was in Roland's heart," said Lestray.

"He really joined your group?"

"He did," said Lestray. "We have no membership rosters nor formal initiations, but he attended our meetings, asked us about our beliefs. He accepted us, and we accepted him. Oh yes, Mr. Targo, he went through everything necessary to be one of the New Judeans. He was, in fact, one of us."

Jason thought Lestray made it so simple, the sanctimonious, silver-tongued bastard. Jason folded his arms, glared at Lestray, and said, "He ate blubber with the Eskimos, too, but that didn't make him Nanook of the North." Then he silently swore at himself and thought he should be talking to these people instead of antagonizing them. Maybe they knew something about his uncle's disappearance.

"He liked us because we aren't as dogmatic as other religions," said the woman. Her voice was as soft as water rippling across rocks. "He liked what we teach."

"We have the true religion," said O'Kelly. His voice was also quiet, but he seemed tense, as if daring someone to contradict him.

Lestray said, "Other religions have much to admire, of course. Many of them have pieces of the truth. We accept much of what the Bible has to say, especially in the stories of the Lost Tribes of Israel. But you would have assumed that much from our name."

He gestured toward his headgear. "Most of all, we live in harmony with nature, as our brothers, the Indians, have always done. We also worship their God, Gitchee Manitou, the lord of the land and forests, but while our Native American brethren have diluted and divided their religion by mixing it

51

with Christianity, our faith has remained pure."

"This cabin," said O'Kelly, "and this land, it's ours."

Jason couldn't resist a smile. "The hell you say!"

Lestray smiled broadly, although his teeth showed through the beard like the fangs of a friendly greyhound. "Jim is a bit obstreperous, but his assertion is correct. Like the true Native American religion, we have a true communal philosophy. When someone joins our order, his worldly goods become part of the New Judeans."

"So this is not your land," said O'Kelly.

Lestray said, "He would have willed it to us."

O'Kelly said, "So it isn't yours."

They reminded Jason of two TV news persons, going back and forth, each with a line on the latest disaster, and the girl is in the background, like the weather person, waiting for her turn.

"It's still his," said Jason. "He isn't officially dead yet. And even if he is, I'm his heir."

"That was not his intention," said Lestray. He put his palms together and bowed slightly.

Jason thought that Lestray must have borrowed that from the Japanese.

"I'm sure you wouldn't want to go against his wishes," Lestray almost whispered.

"You'd better have some good proof of all this," said Jason flatly. "And until you have, get the hell off my land."

Lestray folded his arms and slowly said, "We aren't in a hurry. We understand that Roland hasn't been declared officially dead. Perhaps he has disappeared temporarily. I believe he sometimes was gone for months on expeditions."

"Not without telling me," said Jason. "And he didn't. Yeah, he's gone, but he was a tough old bird. I'm not declaring him dead yet. So this land is still his and I'll use it."

52

"And you're welcome to do so," Lestray said, smoothly. "Until it becomes ours, of course."

He motioned to the others, herding them back into the cab of the pickup. Before he climbed back in, he smiled once more at Jason and said, "May the spirit of Gitchee Manitou be with you, brother. Please visit us any time you choose. I hope you will be receptive to our message."

He started the engine, and the truck sputtered around in a turn, then back and forth until it was pointed the way it had come in. Lestray's hand stuck out the window in a last wave as he left.

Jason felt the urge to say that the Judean was mighty nice to let him stay there. If he had to give it up, Lestray and his Native American brethren could divide it. Maybe the Forest Service, the I.R.S., and the Department of Natural Resources would want a piece of it, too. They could fight each other like the Kilkenney cats. He knew none of them could do anything, not while there was even a slim chance that Uncle Roland might still be alive.

Chapter 8

The Round Stone

After the Zinners left, Jason dressed and ate bacon and eggs, washed down with coffee.

Time to do something, he decided.

He drove to Jackpine and found a sporting goods shop on Peavey Street. Inside, a middle-aged clerk showed a welcoming smile. His T-shirt had a cartoon of a musky holding a foaming schooner of beer in each fin. Below, it said, "Born to Fish." He showed interest when Jason filled in the form to buy bullets.

"From Milwaukee, huh?"

Jason nodded.

"You want longs or shorts?"

"Long rifle."

"Hollow nose?"

"No," said Jason.

He bought four boxes. The clerk warned him not to shoot in the national forest, Indian reservation, near cabins, fishermen, loon nests, or farms. He acted as if he'd be happier if Jason went back to Milwaukee to shoot.

Jason hefted the bag of bullets. He'd almost forgotten how heavy even small caliber ones could be.

Outside, the sun beat down on the tourists mobbing

Peavey Street. As he was crowded against the front of the building, he considered going back into the air-conditioned shop to buy a holster. He decided against it. He felt there was something about how a guy carries a gun. It's hidden if you put it into your pocket or stick in your belt under your shirt. Then the weapon gives you a sense of security. Carry it in a holster on the hip and it's too easy to play John Wayne, swaggering and waiting for a chance to match draws with someone.

The gun might not even be much protection. It certainly wasn't as powerful as a steel, broad-tipped arrow shot from a hunting bow with a fifty-pound draw. But the Ruger had the advantage of six shots. And, more importantly, it was a gun. But who would he need it against? Probably not Bobby Whitefish.

Time to find out more about him and his friends.

Deputy Mink, again at his desk, nodded as Jason entered. "Ah, Mr. Targo. You're back." He gestured to a chair. "Somehow, I'm not surprised to see you."

Jason sat in the captain's chair and said nothing for a moment, wondering if he should confide in the Indian, and yet knowing that Mink might have answers.

"You had some visitors this morning," said Mink. "It must have been a surprise. Not a very welcome one, either, I hear."

Jason couldn't help grinning. "How did you hear so soon?"

Mink pointed to the phone. "Heap big Injun smoke signals go over Paleface's wires. As soon as those guys got back from your place, they started bragging about it at the grocery at the reservation mall. Bobby Whitefish was there, but he wasn't the one bragging."

"I can guess who was. Somebody named Willard?"

The inner office door opened and Sheriff Skinner leaned against the jamb, listening. He nodded to Jason.

"Willard Bearclaw," said Mink. "He's been in trouble off and on, with us and the tribal police. Mostly fights, stuff like that. Pushing tourists around when he has the chance, especially if they're at the mall. He insults them, tries to get them to fight. Naturally, they don't want to fight a punk like Willard. They're intimidated by being surrounded by Indians, too, so it makes him feel even tougher."

"He wasn't just playing Indian this morning," said Jason. "He had a heavy bow and hunting arrows. He said something about making me disappear like my uncle did."

Skinner said, "You want to file a complaint against him?"

Jason shrugged. "What good would that do?"

"Not much. It'd be your word against his."

Mink said, "Against six of them, from what I heard."

Skinner said, "That's right. Hell, you know how it is."

Jason knew. He remembered the times he'd answered domestic disturbance calls and found a bloody, bruised woman.

"My husband beat me," she'd said.

"We'll put him in jail," Jason would say.

"He's been there. When he gets out he beats me again."

"You could put him under a peace bond."

"I did. He still beats me."

"You could leave him."

"I can't. He's my husband."

What could he tell her? Run away? It might be her only chance and she wouldn't take it. The next time, someone would be dead; usually not the one who deserved death. Now he experienced the woman's frustration.

"He tries anything," said Skinner, "you could defend yourself. Then we might have to arrest you for trying to save your own life. That's how the system works."

"We could talk to Willard," said Mink. "I could, I guess."

Skinner agreed. "You could. It'd just be going through the motions. You'd probably have to give him a couple of raps on the head to get his attention, and then he'd sue you for trying to make him listen. For sure, we don't have enough on him to bring him in."

Jason rose. "Well, I'll be leaving. I wanted to find out about him, and I guess I did."

Mink, who had been doodling on a scratch pad, looked up quickly. "Leaving to where?"

"Not Milwaukee, back to the cabin."

Skinner grunted. "Good luck. There's not much we can do to help you, not way out there. And except for the lake, you're almost surrounded by Indian land. They have jurisdiction there."

"In other words," said Jason grimly, "if I'm dead, you can look for Willard Bearclaw first."

"That's about the size of it," Skinner agreed. "And if it happens out there, well, like I told you before, you may never be found, so take care of yourself."

"Because you can't," said Jason as he left.

The doctor in Milwaukee had said, "Get exercise, but use your common sense. Walking is good, and arm exercises. Just don't try to be a contortionist."

While Jason lunched on a corned beef sandwich and coffee at the Shantyboy Tavern, he considered a visit to the Jackpine Country Club for some putting practice. He liked golf, but he didn't want to try the driving range. He imagined his backbone tightening like a wrung dishrag.

Instead, he took the scenic route through the Jackpine National Forest in a roundabout way back to the cabin. As he drove in and out of tree shade, the sunshine flashed in his eyes with the sensation of psychedelic blinking lights.

He couldn't stop thinking about his trip to the newspaper office, and Erica Chamberlain, and how her hair hung down to her shoulders like a blond waterfall. He remembered her small, almost secretive, grin before she said something funny. It had been months since he'd spent any time with a woman, even socially. Except the nurses, of course. When white uniforms began to look sexy, he knew he had to get out of the hospital. No wonder he was getting horny thoughts about Erica. He didn't even know if she was married.

His foot hit the brake pedal when he suddenly realized the dark blob ahead in the middle of the road was no shadow. The car screeched and slewed to a stop crosswise. Not more than twenty feet in front of him, a dog, probably a German shepherd, stood on four widespread legs and dared the car to come closer. Then he realized that was a wolf, a timber wolf, from the size of it. Skinner had mentioned a pack in the area. Jason slowly backed up and straightened the car. As he looked in the rear view mirror, he saw a car approaching. He flicked on the hazard flashers and drove slowly into the other lane. As he passed the wolf, it stared in curiosity or defiance. Jason thought it might be hunger. The wolf looked damned near big enough to eat the car.

As he drove farther, he looked again in the rear view mirror. The wolf had disappeared.

He thought, the Department of Natural Resources is so uptight they won't even let people clean the weeds out of the lakes. They'd probably want to execute him if he ran over an endangered species. He resolved to keep his mind on his driving.

As he drove into the parking area, he watched for signs that Bobby Whitefish or his friends had been there. At the cabin, everything seemed the same as before. Willard hadn't even returned to get his arrow, for it still stuck in the door. Yet, Jason couldn't be sure. He drove forward and parked beside Roland's pickup, took the bag of bullets, and got out of the car. He walked to the front door, then moved around the corner to the north side and looked through the window. He couldn't see anybody inside. He went around to the other side. No one there. A few boats floated offshore, none of them close, and the fishermen seemed innocent and disinterested.

He returned to the front door, unlocked it and entered cautiously. Still no one inside. He walked in, looked around, and sighed with relief. Apparently no one had been there. He put the bag of bullets on the kitchen table and pulled out the dresser drawer. There, where he'd left it, was the little six-shooter. He picked it up and held it lightly in his hand, then opened the loading gate. The cylinder was clean, and he smelled the faint odor of oil. He opened one of the boxes, thumbed six shells into the cylinder and snapped the gate shut.

He decided he probably couldn't hit a barn wall if he was inside. He aimed the Ruger at a knot on the pine paneling. His arm wavered after a second and he let it sag to his side. Then he put his right fist in his left palm and tried again. Not much steadier. He'd need more arm exercise before he could hold his aim.

He looked under the sink and pulled out a large, flattened paper bag. He found a few thumb tacks in the desk and a thick-tipped Magic Marker with enough ink to make a thumb-sized bull's-eye in the middle of the bag.

He stuck the gun into his waistband, put the box of bullets in a pocket, walked outside and looked at the woods on the north and south. The last time he'd been at the cabin, no one had been living close by. Best to make sure, he decided.

Eeeny, meeny, and he picked the north side and walked into the woods, slogging through vines and underbrush as he searched for signs of any other humans. The new growth of pines was randomly planted, not in rows like some reforested areas. This was like Longfellow's forest primeval, but the pines didn't murmur. Not even sounds of boat motors penetrated the woods. His footsteps were muffled by the layer of brown pine needles on the forest floor. When he stopped and listened, he heard birds. Not many, not loud, just a few chirps from somewhere in the branches.

He thought he might be on the property to the north, but he saw no people, no houses. He walked back to the parking area. If he stayed by the cabin and shot to the north, it would be safe enough. Even if a bullet ricocheted off a tree, it wouldn't go far before it hit another one. He tacked the bag to the side of a tree trunk and stepped ten paces away.

He raised the Ruger, aimed, and fired as the sights came in line with the target. He felt the light jolt in his hand and saw the gun barrel jump. The bag didn't move, and he didn't see a hole in it. He shot and missed again. He used the two-handed stance, held his breath, cocked the hammer, aimed, and slowly pulled the trigger while he tried to keep the sights on the target. This time he hit the lower right hand corner of the bag. Better. He shot three more times, reloaded, and fired until only two bullets remained in the box.

When he walked to the tree, he saw three holes in the spot.

Other holes were scattered around it, and he found shredded bark where more bullets hit. His ears clanged and his arm quivered from tiredness, the recoil, or both.

As he turned to go back to the cabin, he noticed a round stone almost buried in the grass. It was head-sized, a dirty brown, and slightly flattened on the top. As he squatted to look at it, he knew it wasn't a rock, but the upper part of a skull. The eye sockets gaped vacantly at him. A piece was broken out of the top, and a dime-sized hole was in the left temple.

The front teeth were large, with a gap between the incisors.

It was Uncle Roland's skull.

He rocked back on his heels, and felt tears flow from his eyes and roll down his cheeks.

Chapter 9

Cursed Land

Jason felt reluctant to leave the skull, as if some mystical being had brought it and might take it away. He stuck the revolver in his waistband, covered it with his shirt, waved a fisherman in, and asked him to go to the nearest phone to call the sheriff. The fisherman, a red-faced, thick man with doubting eyes, insisted on seeing the skull before he gave up his spot above a log fish crib at the bottom of the lake. But what the hell, he finally said, he wasn't catching anything anyway, and he was almost out of beer. He pushed off in his boat and putted away, clearly glad for an excuse to get back to the bar at the lodge. Jason had the impression that the skull story would be much more exciting than tales of fish he didn't catch.

Jason put the gun back in the drawer, sat on the cot, and mourned. After a half hour, he decided to make coffee. He couldn't suppress a grin as he thought, suddenly and inanely, if he'd known cops were coming, he'd have bought some doughnuts.

An hour later, two sheriff's department cars arrived and parked behind Roland's truck. Sheriff Skinner climbed out of the driver's side as Erica Chamberlain got out of the passenger side. Deputy Mink, carrying an evidence kit, emerged from the other car.

Skinner came forward. "Sorry, I hear you found something."

"Yes, me too," said Erica.

Jason nodded and led them to the skull. Skinner stood with his hands behind his back, rocking back and forth as he looked at it. "I assume you didn't move it."

"I haven't touched it at all."

Mink asked, "Find anything else?"

"I didn't look."

"We will," said Skinner. "Pretty sure we won't find anything else, though. It wasn't here the last time we searched. That was after the snow melted. I don't think we'd have missed this."

Mink said, "That first time, there was so much snow that we couldn't tell what was under it. But we're pretty sure his body wasn't here then."

Erica asked, "With all the snow, how could you tell?"

Skinner stared at his feet and muttered, "Aw, hell, I don't like to talk about that sort of stuff."

Jason knew the answer. "I'll have coffee for anybody wants it," he said.

As he walked away, Jason heard Skinner tell Erica, "If the body had been here, the bears or coyotes would have found it first and pawed up the snow."

Jason put on the coffee pot, then looked out the window and watched Skinner and Erica search while Mink measured and took pictures. When the coffee finished perking, Jason stuck his head out the door and shouted, "Coffee! And a beer for anybody who wants it!"

"A beer would be good," said Skinner as he and Erica entered.

They sat at the table while Jason poured two coffees and handed Skinner a can of Leinie. He set his cap on the table and shook his head when Jason gestured to offer a glass for the beer.

Jason said, "I assumed Roland was dead. If he was alive, he would have told me where he was. But, damn it! To find his skull right there! I thought I was used to that kind of thing, but I'm not. Not when it's somebody I loved."

"I know," said Skinner. "I keep thinking of you as a cop, but I'm sure this is tough on you when it gets this personal. I got to ask you, though, did you notice the scratches?"

"On Unk's, on the skull? No."

"Not surprised. You're too emotional right now to notice stuff like that. There's some deep grooves on the top." He put his fingers on his own head to demonstrate. "They're from claws or teeth, I think. Maybe both. Something powerful and probably big. Bear or maybe wolf. They don't usually kill people, but in the middle of winter, when they're hungry they might find somebody who's already, well, you know."

Erica reached over, put her hand on Jason's and whispered, "I'm sorry."

He nodded, not wanting to say anything. He didn't know why she was here, aside from the obvious reason of getting a story for the paper. She could have sent a reporter, or maybe she didn't have one on the staff. This wasn't Milwaukee, where he could expect to find people from TV or the papers when something like this happened. He didn't want his personal life in the Jackpine paper, but maybe there wasn't that much to report, just the bare outline of finding the skull.

"We'll need formal identification," said Skinner. "Your word is enough for now, but I suppose it'll be official when the crime lab in Madison checks the teeth with the prof's dental records."

They heard the quick toot of a horn outside. Jason rose and looked out the window.

A stooped, thin figure climbed out of a truck parked in the grass under a pine tree. A younger-looking Indian wearing overalls climbed out of the driver's side.

Skinner exclaimed, "I'll be damned! It's Charley Rogers."

Mink suddenly appeared at the back door. He held something behind his back and avoided Jason's eyes. "Like we figured, I didn't find anything else. Anyway, I got it."

The skull, Jason assumed.

Skinner said, "Okay. Put it in the car. How could Charley find out?"

"The tribal police listen to our radio band, don't they?"

Skinner nodded. "So they would have heard me call you in so we could come out here. And somebody there would have told Charley. Might as well go on back. Charley and me, us, we'll all have a talk, that's all. It's not like we need an interpreter."

Mink grinned. "You talked me into it, silver-tongued Paleface. I'll start this moving through the system. Come to think of it, I'm hungry, too, and I didn't get coffee or beer. See you in town."

He held out his hand to Jason. "Sorry we have to meet again this way." He paused a few seconds, thinking, and then added, "With your uncle gone, well, that's changed your situation here, hasn't it? About the land, and you staying here."

Jason shook Mink's hand, but felt some anger and resentment rise against the deputy.

"Well, damned if I'm going to be pushed around," he blurted. "It's me who'll decide what to do."

"Oh, I figured that," said Mink. "I guessed you weren't the kind to be pushed. But from now on, if I were you, I'd be watching careful, front and back."

He nodded to Erica, touched his hat brim with a finger in casual salute, and left. As he opened the door, Jason saw

Charley Rogers approaching.

A battered cowboy hat, pulled low, hid and shaded his eyes. He seemed to be blind, for he stared at the ground and poked at it with a cane, prodding as he tested each step.

Some time ago, his nose had been flattened so it seemed to be missing. His lined face reminded Jason of a giant brown raisin. His mouth was a horizontal slash across his face. He seemed to be incredibly old, yet Jason knew he was about ten years older than Roland.

The younger man hovered close behind, not helping Charley, but ready to catch him if he stumbled.

As Jack passed, he said, "Hello, Mr. Rogers."

"Who the hell are you?"

"Jack Mink."

"Ah, the police." Charley nodded. It was enough greeting, apparently, for Mink kept on walking to the police car. He turned to open the door and Jason caught a glimpse of a plastic bag being carefully placed in the back seat. Mink closed the door and walked out of sight toward the lake, probably to get the evidence kit.

Charley stepped slowly and carefully until he apparently saw the shapes of people in front of him, then stopped.

"Hello, Mr. Rogers," said Jason. "Come on in."

"Who are you?" asked Charley as he entered, feeling his way through the doorway.

"Jason Targo."

"Ah, Ahmeek's boy."

"His nephew."

"I know that, but I always thought of you as his boy. You were, really. He raised you. You belonged to him."

His head swiveled as if he could see every face in the cabin. "Who else is here?"

"Erica Chamberlain," said Jason, "from the paper."

"I know who she is," Charley grunted. "Howard, here, my grandson, he reads it to me every week, at least as much as he thinks I ought to know. Is she your woman?"

"I'm nobody's woman," said Erica. Her tone wasn't angry, but an almost unconscious imitation of his frankness.

"I'm here, too," said Skinner.

"The sheriff. I recognize your voice."

"I'm sorry I didn't call you," said Jason. "I meant to."

"But you couldn't. I still don't have a damn phone. And you didn't have the time. I know. You've been busy. I heard of what happened since you came here. I'm sorry too."

Jason held out a hand and gently took hold of Charley's elbow, but the old man waved him off.

"I don't need that much help yet." He reached out, felt a chair, and sat. "Is this place like it was before?"

"The way it was when I saw it the last time," said Jason.

"I could see better when I saw it the last time. These damned eyes, they go fast. The doctors at the clinic say they can help me, but why? It's almost time for me to go anyway, and I think I've seen everything I want to see. Besides, what is there to see now? The young men are wild. I was a young man, and I was wild, so I've seen that. Ahmeek helped me to be calm when it was necessary. He taught me not to butt my head against stone walls."

He found the table and rested his hands on it. "I'll have a beer. Any beer. Or water. Howard will have water. He may ask for something stronger, but don't give it to him. He's driving. A horse would know where to go but a truck doesn't, so I need him sober."

Howard grinned and shrugged. He was probably a few years younger than Jason, slim, with a dark tan complexion and without prominent cheekbones, a typical Algonquian face. His shaggy black hair, almost glossy, stuck out from under a Milwaukee Brewers cap.

As Jason popped open a can of Leinenkuegel, he gestured to it, looking at Howard. The grandson grinned again and shook his head. "No water either, thanks."

"I'm sorry for what has happened," Charley said, "and for my part in it. I have much to answer for, in this life and the next."

"You had no part in this," said Jason as he put the beer on the table.

"I'm to blame for what has happened." His nose twitched and he reached unerringly for the beer. He picked it up and took a deep drink, then wiped his mouth with his sleeve. "When the Whites took our land to make the lake, they wanted to pay us almost nothing. We lived as we had for many years, in huts with dirt floors. We had little to eat. And we were sick, always sick. When you're poor and dirty and sick, a little money seems like very much. But Ahmeek knew our land was valuable, and he would not see us cheated. Many of us were. Some sold their land and spent the money. Some drank it up. Some moved in with those who still had land."

He took another drink. "Ahmeek found lawyers in Ashland who told us the right things to do. Then if we had to sell our land, at least we got a fair price. But some of the young people today think that no price was fair, that we still own the world."

He shook his head. "But we don't. Strangers bought our land, and some of them live among us today. There is nothing we can do about it now, and I tell our young men they should not try, for it was a trade, just as our people used to trade Lake Superior copper for Everglades alligator teeth."

He sighed. His lower lip quivered and he almost seemed to be crying, but he took another drink of beer instead. He pointed to the floor. "This piece of land belonged to me. I gave it to Ahmeek. I thought I did him a favor, for none of our people ever came to this part of the lake. But if you give something to someone, especially one who is your friend, you should give something of value. This land was worthless to me. Less than worthless, for it is cursed. I thought that could not affect the professor, for he wasn't one of the FirstMen. I was wrong, and I did a shameful thing when I gave him this land."

The palm of his hand slapped the table, almost upsetting the beer can.

"This land was cursed here, right here! It happened more than a hundred years ago, even before this lake was here. This is where the windigo was!"

Chapter 10

1870, in the Season of Bibon

As Isaac Broadbow tramped past pine boughs sagging from snow layers, he worried about what might happen.

In the season of Migwunong, when skies cleared and snow melted, the Blackrobes had come to the hunting grounds of the FirstMen and built a stone and log church where they worshipped the Jesus God with strange chants and smoky smells. After that, both Jesus and Gitchee Manitou turned their faces from the FirstMen.

Now, in Onabingizis, snow-crusted month, the tribe's storehouses, once packed with dried meat and berries, were almost empty. The agent gave the FirstMen no food, and they suspected he sold it to the storekeepers in Jackpine. Even worse, snares caught no rabbits, and bears stayed away from log traps. Wolves learned not to snap at the baited hooks hanging from trees.

That winter, the dreaded, withered Bukadawin, the spirit of starvation, visited the camps. Three days ago, the kettles above the fires had begun to sway, although there was no wind.

Isaac Broadbow worried about that as he tramped through the frozen forest. He worried about his wife, too.

She stayed at home, sat and stared into the fire and talked

of the windigo she had seen in the forest. It was a skeleton of ice, she said, as tall as a pine tree. An icy heart throbbed inside its ribs. It knocked trees aside as it walked through the forest and picked up rabbits, mice, even bears. It crunched their bones with its icicle teeth and swallowed them. Even as the animals disappeared into the windigo's bones, it hungered for more.

Isaac became sad and fearful when his wife claimed that the spirit of the windigo had entered her, for he knew what happened to people who were cursed with that terrible fate.

It was beginning already. She refused the few shreds of food that Isaac could offer. She told him she was a windigo, and they would have to pour hot fat down her throat to melt her heart of ice so the windigo spirit would be driven out. The children, only five and six years old, didn't know why their mother acted so strange. Isaac warned them to stay away from her, that she had gone windigo.

The same thing had happened many years ago, also in the season of bibon, when snow covered the ground and animals hid from the hunters. Isaac had heard the story when he was young, as it was told by the people of the Wolf Clan.

A man had found no food for weeks. Then he refused to hunt or eat or sleep. He stared into the fire and moaned. He said his wife and mother-in-law looked like fat beavers. He said he would kill them if the windigo was not driven from his body. His family knew that pouring boiling oil down his throat would drive out the windigo, but it would also kill him.

They sent for a *djasakid,* a juggler man who could cure him by using magic. But it was a long trip on snowshoes to where the juggler man lived.

Before the juggler man arrived, the man walked out into the snow one night and disappeared. No one ever saw him again. No one found his bones. Maybe he threw himself into the snow and froze. Maybe he went into the woods and killed himself with his knife. He would do that so he couldn't kill his wife and mother-in-law.

Or maybe he went somewhere else to kill other people's wives and mothers-in-law, and the people there poured boiling oil down his throat and then chopped the heart of ice from his chest.

Usually only the men went windigo, but sometimes a woman did, especially one who had given up the ways of women. Now Isaac's wife refused to sew rabbit fur leggings for him, or to chew deerskin to make it soft for moccasins, and so his feet felt cold in his leather boots as he waded through the snow.

Isaac knew no juggler man could help her. Juggler men were weak now, their powers waning like the moon. The FirstMen were turning from them and going more to the White doctors who stuck sticks of glass in their mouths, listened through tubes to their breathing, and said there were no such things as windigos.

But maybe Isaac could still save his wife. He had walked far to spend hours in a fish tent on a lake, peering through a hole in the ice. And then, finally, a musky swam by. It was almost as long as Isaac's arm, and fat. Isaac impaled it with one lunge of his long, three-pronged spear. Soon the fish would be boiled over the fire, and they would all eat. It would be almost as good as beaver.

The sun was behind the trees when he came to his wigwam of bark-covered bent poles. Ahead, Isaac saw the glow of the fire inside. He knew his wife and children would be huddled around it to keep warm.

When he pulled aside the deerskin and entered, he saw his wife sitting on a blanket, facing the fire. Her elbows stuck out, and her head bobbed up and down.

She was eating.

Good, Isaac thought. She found something to eat. Perhaps she would share it with the children. But he didn't see them. Maybe they had tired of sliding the wooden snow snake and gone out to hunt. They couldn't kill a large animal, but they might throw sticks and hit a rabbit.

When his wife turned around, he saw her red teeth and the blood dripping from the corners of her mouth. She held up what she was eating, offering to share her feast, and he knew what had happened to the children.

He screamed in anger and raised the fishing spear.

Chapter 11

Rattling the Cage

After Charley finished the story of Isaac Broadbow and his windigo wife, the others sat silently for a few minutes, as if some psychic residue of terror and death lingered to cast gloom on the cabin and its occupants. No one felt modern nor superior enough to disparage or mock Charley's tale.

Then he said, "Would any just God permit such a thing to happen? Maybe something like that doesn't belong in any religion. I should have thought of that before I gave this land to Ahmeek. I should have treated this land like God did Sodom, sowed it with salt to make it barren forever. Jason, I am sorry."

He rose and walked out the door to his truck. The others followed. The sheriff got in his cruiser, talked and listened on the radio for a few minutes, then climbed out, frowning.

"Sorry, Erica, but I can't bring you back right away. Got a call from Fish Heaven Lodge, over on the east side of the lake. Two fishermen fought about who lost the biggest bass. Hell of a thing to fight about! Anyway, the one started it, he's drunk and out cold at the bar. He got whacked with a canoe paddle and tied up with twenty-pound line. I'll have to pick him up, throw him in the back seat, bring him in, maybe even hose the puke off him first. Pardon my French."

Jason told her, "I'll bring you in."

"That'd be nice," said Erica. "Sharing a ride with a stinky drunk doesn't sound appetizing."

Howard backed the pickup around to get out of the crowded parking area. After he and Charley drove away, Skinner turned his car around and left.

Jason and Erica smelled the faint exhaust of the vehicles and, after the sounds of the motors died away, they heard rustles of small animals in the brush and, out of sight on the lake, the eerie wail of a loon.

"Calling the mate," said Erica, quietly. "I hope the other one makes it back to the nest. Sometimes they don't. It could be caught by a fisherman's lure, or a musky. Sometimes a boat gets too close, and the loon protects the nest by screaming and flapping its wings until its heart quits."

Jason felt almost that tired himself.

"Well, the suspense is over," he said. "It's what I've been expecting, so it's almost a relief that it finally happened. You want a beer or something before you go back?"

She shook her head.

He said, "I heard what you told Charley."

She seemed puzzled. "What was that?"

"About being nobody's woman," he answered, grinning.

"He got me pissed off. Him and his 'Me buck, you squaw' attitude. By now some squaw should have taught him a lesson, like maybe she wasn't just a squaw any more."

"They couldn't do much teaching back when Charley got married. If a wife got uppity, her husband could cut her nose off, and the other men would say it served her right."

"The good old days," she muttered, grimacing.

After Jason locked the cabin, they climbed into the Honda and he drove toward Jackpine.

"Maybe you'd like a drink in town," he said, "even if it's just coffee."

"I'd better not. I want to get my notes straight while they're fresh. Maybe I'll even write the story tonight." When she put a hand on his arm, a light tingle flowed through him. She murmured, "Some other night, I wouldn't mind it at all. You know where to find me. No, I forgot, you don't, not after the office is closed. I'm in the phone book. Just call before so I can be sure I'm free."

"No problem. I wouldn't want you to break a date."

"I usually have a date to cover a chamber of commerce meeting or half a dozen other things. Jackpine isn't exactly Times Square at night, even in summer, but people find things to do. They just aren't very exciting."

Jason remembered moments of excitement on the streets of Milwaukee. Somehow, they always seemed to include violence and blood. "I've seen excitement. I'll take dull any time."

As they drove along the road, the car's lights drilled a tunnel though the trees. "Maybe a little excitement," he said. "Have you ever been to the Wilderness of Zin?"

"Just once, when they first got here, and I did an interview with Lestray. Why? Do you want to go there now?"

He grinned. "I guess it would be fun, well, very mild excitement to go to their place, see what they've got, maybe rattle their cage. And I think I should have a witness, somebody not on their side. We wouldn't stay long."

"I really do have to work tonight," she said, hesitantly.

"Word of honor." He hoped he could keep his promise.

He reached the main highway, turned, and drove carefully, looking for the Zinners' mailbox and fallen sign. Fortunately, he drove slowly enough to avoid the porcupine that waddled down the center line, daring any car to invade its highway. Beside the mailbox, a two-lane blacktop road went south. The Zinners must have votes, Jason thought, or some pull somewhere. But then, maybe the county keeps all its roads in good shape, not just the ones to boat landings and resorts. It was only a couple of miles to the Wilderness, but it seemed longer, perhaps because he drove slowly to avoid surprising any animals. On the left of the road he saw a small sign, white painted on a plain board, "Wilderness of Zin," and an arrow pointing to a dirt road on the left. The paved road question was easily answered, for he saw a boat landing ahead, an asphalt parking area that sloped down and into the water. Dim boat lights moved on the lake.

He turned left and drove about a block, he guessed, to a grassy area, turned off the lights and parked beside several cars and trucks, including Lestray's pickup. Ahead, he saw a flickering glow in the woods. Muttering noises, punctuated with what seemed to be drumbeats, filtered through the trees.

He and Erica walked along a path toward the glow for about two hundred feet and emerged in a clearing. About fifty people sat on logs clustered in two groups that faced each other across a fire. They wore buckskin suits, probably Indian costumes. Their faces showed like pale polka dots against the dark background of trees. The clothing looked hot and uncomfortable, but probably gave some protection against mosquitoes. A drummer sat in front of one group and pounded a staggered rhythm of eight beats, while the other drummer hammered three times, paused, then another three times. The result was a throbbing cacophony.

When he felt a hand on his arm, tugging somewhat roughly, he turned, tensed and ready to strike. The man beside him stepped back with his hands in the air, palms peacefully outward. He was about six feet tall, with bulk that didn't seem to be flabby flat. He had dark hair and a smashed nose. When he smiled, Jason saw the gap where a front tooth had been. He wore buckskin, like the others, and a feathered headband.

He asked, "Who are you, brother?"

Another figure appeared out of the darkness and said, "Why, it's Mr. Targo."

"Hello, Lestray," said Jason.

"This is Lyle Brennan," Lestray said.

Lyle folded his arms and stared at Jason. The smile stayed on his face, but it seemed more polite than friendly.

"You must forgive him," Lestray murmured. "He watches out for us, and I make sure he isn't too zealous."

He turned to Lyle, who seemed more suspicious than zealous.

"This is Mr. Targo," said Lestray, as if the big man hadn't heard the greeting.

"Yeah, him," Lyle grunted.

"And who is this?" asked Lestray.

"Erica Chamberlain," said Erica, "from the newspaper. I interviewed you a few months ago."

"Now I remember," Lestray murmured. He turned back to Jason. "What brings you here tonight?"

"You invited me, remember? I know it's sort of late, but we were driving by and I had an impulse to drop in. Hope you don't mind."

He thought his excuse sounded as phony as Lestray's welcome.

"I don't mind at all," said Lestray, with a wide, white smile. "Lyle, you can go back to your group."

Lyle glared at Erica and Jason and silently padded away.

"Lyle is a recent convert," said Lestray as they walked toward the fire. "They tend to be more sensitive to people they feel are outsiders. Which you are, in a sense, not being one of us like Roland was."

As they approached the fire, Jason saw about fifty people seated on logs. On one side, people swayed and chanted a repetition of "Oh, hear us, Gitchee Manitou." Four people thumped Indian drums to accompany them with a rhythm which Jason suddenly recognized as "Oh, Tannenbaum."

"They call to Gitchee Manitou," Lestray whispered.

"I guessed that much," said Jason. He couldn't resist adding, "Does he ever answer?"

"Gitchee Manitou is neither he nor she," said Lestray. "Gitchee Manitou is the spirit residing in each of us, in everything, and so is sexless. However, we pretentious humans like to refer to Gitchee Manitou as he or she, whichever suits our preferences. Gitchee Manitou does not care."

Jason watched Lestray, who showed no hint of a smile. He seemed to be serious.

"Very considerate of Gitchee," said Jason. "Most gods are pretty fussy about what they're called."

"But, to answer your question, Gitchee Manitou sometimes is manifested among us."

Lestray led them to the other side of the clearing, where a group chanted, "Hoongawa, Hoongawa, Hoongawa" in time to the three-beat rhythm of the drum.

Erica asked, "Hoongawa? What's that?"

"It has no meaning. It does have a somewhat Indian sound, though."

"Maybe," she said, grinning, "but I'm not sure an Indian would appreciate it. It shows about as much as respect as the White actors in *Peter Pan* doing a war dance while they sing 'Ugga wugga wigwam.' "

"Must be related to the Fugawee," said Jason, trying to hide his own grin in the darkness. "You know, the tribe that got its name when it was lost and the chief asked, 'Where the fugawee?' Pardon my French, as the sheriff would say."

"No relation that I know of," said Lestray, as if Jason had been serious. "Hoongawa is merely a word used for clearing the mind so the spirit of Gitchee Manitou can enter."

Jason said, "After a couple of hours of that, I know my mind would be clear. Maybe completely erased."

"What happens when the spirit enters somebody?" asked Erica.

"They behave in whatever way they are affected. Some dance, some sing, some don't move at all."

Erica asked, "Speak in tongues?"

"Sometimes."

Jason thought they even borrowed from the Pentecostals and the Holy Rollers. In the Hoongawa section, a woman stood up.

"I believe it's starting now," said Lestray. "Some are more open to the spirit."

I'll bet they are, thought Jason as he saw the woman glance toward him as she raised her arms.

"Margaret Stuart," said Lestray. "You may remember her."

Jason did, but hadn't recognized her in the middle of the group. She watched him, her hands above her head, palms together, elbows waving, and seemed to hula just for him. As she swayed sinuously, Jason decided her dance was more like a cobra coming out of a basket. Then she unbuttoned her blouse and dropped it to the ground. Her breasts, large and bare, quivered as she moved. Next, she held her arms in front, squeezing the breasts, and her brown nipples poked out stiffly.

Erica gasped and turned away and muttered, "Very interesting."

"It certainly is," said Jason.

"You mean, they certainly are. I should be getting back to the office."

Jason thought, I'll be damned. I think she's offended or maybe even embarrassed.

"As I said," Lestray whispered, "the spirit gets into people in different ways."

Probably not all that gets into Ms. Stuart, Jason thought as he stopped a grin.

"That is what we do at some of our ceremonies," said Lestray as they walked back to the cars. "We have other rituals, and we are busy with gardening, building, house-keeping, many other things. It seems as if we spend all summer getting firewood and food ready for winter. And we pray, of course."

Jason recalled the Thomas Nast cartoon of the Tammany Hall vultures saying, "Let us prey."

Lestray continued, "By the way, have you considered our discussion? The matter of the land must be settled sooner or later."

"We've found evidence that my uncle is dead," said Jason.

Lestray stopped as his mouth dropped open. He seemed to consider what to say. Then, "I'm sorry, Jason. Of course, this was not unexpected. May I ask how he died?"

"We don't know."

Lestray said, "Then this does change our situation."

"No, it's as it was before," said Jason, and mentally cursed himself for falling into an unconscious imitation of the leader. "I mean, I'll live in the cabin until I decide what to do."

"Jason, surely that would be inconvenient. You'd have to go so far to get your food. And it would be uncomfortable for someone so used to living in the city."

"I can get along."

"Brother Roland wanted us to have that land, Jason. I'm

sure he'd want you to comply with his wishes."

All of a sudden, he's turned familiar, Jason thought. Now he uses my name all the time, like he wants me to know that he knows me, or maybe to remind me in case I've forgotten who I am. "I don't know about his wishes, but according to the will he wrote, the land is mine. Or it will be after probate."

Lestray said, stiffly, "But Jason, I have witnesses who heard him promise it to us. The land is ours. Gitchee Manitou wants us to have it, and Gitchee Manitou's will cannot be denied."

Creepy, Jason thought as he drove away. Lestray doesn't seem so funny when he threatening me with Gitchee Manitou.

Chapter 12

Inciting a Riot

The next afternoon, Jason again remembered the Buckskin custom of visiting the chief or some tribal elder to show respect and peaceful intentions. And a small tribute was always appropriate.

Buckskin, a small cluster of homes, a gas station, small businesses, and a new shopping mall, could barely be called a village. A few tourists slowly drove through and stayed in their cars as if they were afraid they'd be scalped if they got out. The tribal government had moved to the mall, leaving only the small volunteer fire station behind the vacant one-story brick building that had been the town hall. Jason turned left at the old building and drove about a block, although there were no real blocks, just meandering gravel roads that seemed to intersect accidentally. As Jason parked in front of Charley Rogers' neat, white clapboard house, he saw the flutter of a curtain in a corner window. He got out of the car and the front door opened as Laurel, Charley's middle-aged daughter, stepped out on the porch and stared at him. Then her brown face split in a wide, white smile as she waved and shouted, "Jason!"

He took a six-pack of Walters beer from the front seat and walked to the porch. As they shook hands, she exclaimed, "I haven't seen you for years!"

"No, I guess not. I didn't get up here as much as I used to. How are you?"

"Getting older," she said, smiling. "It's what we all do if we're lucky. I heard you got killed, but then I heard you didn't. Obviously, you didn't."

He grinned. "Obviously."

"Charley isn't here. He went to the mall with Cora."

Cora, his third wife, was about twenty years younger than Charley. Jason never knew for sure if all three had been married to Charley at the same time. They would have been Indian marriages, of course, not sanctioned by church nor government. Jason had never asked, and Uncle Roland had never told him.

"They left a few minutes ago," said Laurel. "They'll be at the IGA doing the weekly shopping, so they'll probably be there for at least an hour."

"At least," said Jason.

"Yes, she does love to cook."

Not only did Cora love to cook, but she loved to shop for food as much as some other women shopped for clothing or shoes.

"I'll look for them there," said Jason. "You've heard about my uncle, I suppose."

She nodded. "I'm sorry about it. I hope it won't cause any more trouble. I heard you already had a run-in with some of our younger ones. I'm sorry Dave was—one of them."

"Dave?"

"Yes, Charley's grandson. I suppose you remember him. Now he calls himself Howling Wolf and runs with that bunch, Bobby Whitefish and Willard Bearclaw and the rest of them. He was at your cabin the other night."

"I didn't recognize him. But the light was bad, too."

"After he found out it was you, he felt bad about being there, so he didn't say who he was. But he was there, and I'm sorry about that. I wish he could be here to apologize himself. If he would. I don't know about the young men these days."

Jason shrugged and said, "As it turned out, there wasn't any trouble."

"That's good."

"I wanted to visit with Charley, but it isn't anything urgent. Here's something for him." He gave her the beer. "I told him yesterday that I'd meant to come by and see him sooner. If I miss him, tell him I was here, will you?"

"Of course."

"I'll go look for them."

"Try the produce section first," she said. "Cora's gone crazy about Indian tacos. We never heard of them until a few years ago, but now, you know, we have a few other Indians living up here. A Navajo or two, and some Sioux."

He laughed. "Sioux? Times have changed."

She smiled. "They have! Why, we haven't scalped a Sioux for years. And now, here they are. And so are Indian tacos. Cora makes them once or twice a week. But you know her. She won't use any sauce from a jar. She'll be looking for a perfect tomato."

Jason waved, got back in the car, and drove north to the Buckskin Mall. He laughed again as he thought about the changing times. The Buckskins and Sioux had fought for years. Finally, about 1750, the Buckskins drove the enemy people from the Great Lakes area. And now, finally, some of them had returned to live as neighbors. They would not be completely accepted, of course. Buckskins considered themselves the only mankind. Just as Navajos called themselves "the People" and the Cheyennes were "Human Beings," Buckskins were "FirstMen." Other races, even Indian tribes, might be equal, but they were not FirstMen.

He turned off the highway at the "Buckskin Mall" sign, pulled into the mall parking lot and climbed out. The mall had no Indian decorations to attract tourists. It looked like any other brick and stucco mall in Ashland or Duluth. As Jason walked inside, he noticed the trading post had a new name.

Otherwise, everything seemed the same. On the wall in front of the trading post, he saw hundreds of notices and fliers for sales, pow-wows, lost dogs, requests for work or baby sitters. A small group of Indians crowded around to read the notices. He heard the usual hum of voices, dings of cash registers, beeps from video games and then, from the other side of the building, loud, raucous laughter, followed by shouts. Everyone looked in that direction, and some wandered over to investigate. Jason walked down the broad hall to follow them. He passed the IGA store, Hardware Hank, a new pizza place, T-shirt salesmen, and the usual small shops. The noises came from the offices of the tribal government near the other end of the building.

The loud voice sounded familiar. "Listen to the words of Gitchee Manitou! He tells you to give up your sinful ways. Join him in worship of all nature!"

Another voice shouted, "Bullshit!"

On tiptoes, Jason could see over the heads of some of the mob in front of him. The tall, lean figure of Lestray stood at the end of the mall. Ed O'Kelly and Lyle Brennan stood beside him. Behind them, a quartet of women faintly sang, "Oh, hear us, Gitchee Manitou."

I'll be damned, Jason thought, grinning. They're Gitchee carolers. Or are they Gitchee Sweet Adelines?

All wore the Zinner buckskin uniforms with headbands and feathers. He didn't see Margaret Stuart, and thought she might be back at the camp, chanting and dancing.

Someone shouted, "You crazy assholes! Get outta here!"

Jason realized it was Willard Bearclaw. He had help, because someone else shouted, "This place is our place."

That sounded familiar. Jason thought it came from the big Indian who'd said, "This land is our land," that night at the cabin.

Bobby Whitefish, standing beside him, whispered, "Knock it off, Wolf. We don't want any trouble."

The big one looked around belligerently. "Whatta ya mean, no trouble. I ain't causin' no trouble, man. It's these fucks doin' it."

"Crazy assholes," Willard repeated.

Jason thought, Wolf? Could that big loudmouth be Charley's grandson? If so, he'd changed a lot since Jason last saw him.

Lyle stepped forward, almost nose to nose with Willard, glaring at him, snarling into his face.

"Who you calling crazy?"

Willard gulped and backed away, but Wolf stepped between them. He was as large and thick as Lyle, and as threatening. "We are!" He turned and pointed to Jason. "And you, too, you're all a bunch of crazy fucks, coming here to make trouble."

Others stared at Jason, and Willard pushed his way through the crowd. He asked, "You still on our land?"

"It's my land," said Jason, quietly.

"Big city cop from Milwaukee," Willard grunted. "You ain't got a gun, you ain't got no club, you ain't tough at all. Just a chickenshit pig."

Jason knew it was no place for a brawl, and remembered the bruised nerve in his back. Be damned if he would spend more months in traction, he decided. Besides, it took more than a few names to make him mad. He put his hands behind his back to demonstrate his peacefulness.

Bobby leaned forward. As he spoke, smoke from the cigarette that dangled from his lips puffed into Willard's face. "I told you before. Lay off him." He gestured to Jason. "This man was my friend, and as far as I'm concerned, he still is unless he says different."

Willard turned to Bobby. "He's a Goddamn Paleface. I told you that before, Bobby. None of them's any friend of ours."

He reached out, grabbed Jason's shirt, and started to pull him forward. Jason had been expecting some hostile movement. He kept his hands behind his back, but his foot lashed out and the toe scraped Willard's shin.

"Sumbitch!" Willard screeched and bent over to grab his leg, massaging it as he swayed back and forth on the other one, trying to keep his balance.

Bobby grabbed Willard and pushed him away. He hopped back, leaned against the wall, and continued to rub his leg.

Bobby snarled, "Stupid shit! Leave him alone. He could of knocked your head off. You're lucky he didn't. I damn sure would of."

A murmur rose behind them, and Jason felt, rather than heard, the crowd move. It parted as Charley Rogers stepped through and stopped in front of Howling Bear.

"Dave!" Charley's voice was quiet, but with a menacing authority.

His grandson shrank back for a second, avoiding the old man's wrath, but then saw the smirks on the faces of his friends. "That's not my name now," he said. "I'm Howling Wolf."

"You're a disgrace to our people," said Charley, quietly. "You're a disgrace to your clan and to our family. I am ashamed to call you my grandson."

Howling Wolf muttered, "Well, don't then. Go fuck your-self."

He had no chance to evade Charley's cane. As it swung up, the tip caught Wolf in the crotch and, when he bent over, clutching himself, the cane rose quickly and slammed across his shoulders.

"Hey, that's enough!"

It was a new voice now, and two tribal policemen came out of the crowd. One was tall and lean, the other shorter. They wore khaki uniforms and cowboy hats.

"Shit," Willard whispered. "It's the cowboys."

The short man reached up, plucked the cigarette from Bobby's mouth, threw it to the floor, and stepped on it. "You can't read 'No Smoking' signs?"

The tall one reached out casually to Willard and grabbed his shirt front. Willard still stood on one foot, rubbing his shin, so it was easy for the officer to fling him to the floor. The officer, his face impassive as stone, moved on to stand beside Lyle. "You. Back where you were."

Lyle glared at him, then slowly backed away to stand be-side Lestray again.

"And you people," the smaller cop told the Zinners, "out!"

Lestray said, "We have a right to be—"

"No!" The officer's exclamation interrupted him. "You don't have a right to be a damned nuisance. We can charge you with trespass, disturbing the peace. Hell, we could charge you with inciting a riot."

"We're peaceful people," said O'Kelly. "We just want to worship in our own way."

The smaller cop said, "Then don't do it here. This isn't a church. It's a shopping center, and I think maybe you came here shopping for a busted head."

The tall one pointed to the door behind the Zinners. "There's the door. We don't want you going out through all these people."

Lestray opened his mouth to protest, saw the expressions on the faces around him and kept silent. Lyle muttered something no one heard. He didn't seem very peaceful, but Lestray gently moved him and O'Kelly toward the back of the mall. "The heathens reject our gospel," he said.

The taller cop said, "You can talk, but you're still leaving."

As the Zinners backed toward the door, the crowd watched silently.

The other officer pointed to Willard, then to Bobby, then to the other door. Bobby and his friends, glaring sullenly, silently walked out.

"Jason, I'm sorry this happened," said Charley, holding out his hand.

Jason shook the old man's hand. "You saw me? Your eyes are getting better or they aren't as bad as you think they are."

"Each person has a different presence, a different shape, even if it's fuzzy," said Charley, grinning. "I recognize yours."

"I'm glad," said Jason. "I wanted to visit with you, but we don't have to do it right now. I know you're busy."

"I'm an old man. I have nothing left to do but die. And I can wait for that. Come for supper tomorrow night. Cora will fix Indian tacos. That's what they're called, even though they are made by the Navajos. But she likes to make them, and I eat a few. We can talk while you eat with us. If we get to eat. If Cora chooses the food. She still hasn't moved past the green peppers."

"I'll try to be there. I'll call."

"In the meantime, be careful. Dave and his friends thought you were weak and vulnerable. Now they know differently. They may leave you alone. But we don't know what they will do. Perhaps they themselves don't know. They will not listen to the elders, and there is no one else to teach them either the old ways or the new ones."

Chapter 13

Fright Night

As Jason drove away from the mall, he decided he needed to know more about what had happened long ago at Windigo Pond. He drove to Jackpine, parked on Peavey Street, and walked into the newspaper office. Blanche had the phone stuck to her ear again, so he mouthed "Erica" and pointed a finger at the inner office. Blanche smiled and waved at the door. Jason stuck his head into the office. She sat at her desk, and he saw she was old-fashioned enough to use a pencil to correct a computer printout. She looked up, smiled, and the room brightened.

"I came to get some information," he said. "I guess you're busy."

"Sorry."

He smiled back and impulsively said, "Maybe we might have supper. You asked for advance notice, but I'm sort of isolated at the lake without a phone."

She smiled. "I know. The primitive life. Thanks for the offer, but I can't tonight. I'm having supper with Blanche."

"Okay," he said, nodding.

"It's really business. She likes to cook and talk, and she can tell me more about what's going on than I can ever find out sitting behind this desk."

"Some other time, maybe," said Jason.

"It's just dinner, though."

Jason smiled again. "Then you might be free after that?"

"I think so. You're not busy?"

"It's been hectic since I got here. And then yesterday, what with finding Uncle Roland, well, that's over now. At least I can stop wondering what happened. But it was a shock. He was like . . ." He paused and cleared his throat. "He was really my father, after my parents died. But I guess I've been grieving for him since January. Finding his skull was sort of a relief. There's nothing can be done now, not until I make arrangements for some kind of services. But no, I'm not busy tonight, and I need a change."

"Okay," she said. "There isn't much going on in town, though. You can't expect excitement on a Sunday night. It all happens Friday and Saturday nights at the Shantyboy."

"The Shantyboy? I thought you said it was closed."

"The old one, but the owner got lonesome, I guess, and started another one a few blocks away on Peavey, near the country club. This one's just a plain brick building, not nearly as colorful as the old place. On weekends he has country-western bands. The Hog Callers, Bug Stompers, or something like that. But tonight? Maybe you can go watch the Zinners dance. You might see something that's really, well, you know."

"Don't say it," he interrupted, smiling again.

"Titillating. Couldn't resist it. I don't know what's at the movie theater tonight, but around here we see whatever's playing, watch TV, or rent a video. Sometimes we even read."

Jason said, "Want to see the movie? I'm not fussy about what I watch."

She scribbled on a scrap of paper and gave it to him.

"Here's my address. I'm upstairs. Just ring the bell. Is seven okay? The movie always starts at seven-thirty."

"Seven should be fine."

After leaving the office, he walked across the street to a restaurant, Muskyville, where customers ate at picnic tables on a flagstone patio under a large sign that advertised, "Beer, Burgers, Brats and More!" He ate a lunch of a corned beef sandwich with fries, pickles, and hot German potato salad.

He'd meant to ask Erica about local history. That idea was sidetracked for now, but he could look in another place. He walked back across the street and a block south to the Jackpine Public Library. Jason walked inside, up a short flight of stairs, and entered the circulation room. It had a high ceiling and shelves filled with books. The librarian behind the desk was middle-aged and gray-haired, a grim-friendly combination. He suspected she was a school teacher, summer moonlighting. She looked at him as if she'd never seen a stranger there before.

"I'm interested in local history," he said, smiling. "Do you have some books on it?"

She smiled carefully, as if her face might shatter, and said there were a few. "Small ones, almost pamphlets, mostly written by people in the local historical society. And the local paper used to run a history column."

Jason mentally kicked himself. When he'd lived here before, he occasionally read Hester Meldon's columns in the paper. He should have remembered them.

"But she hasn't been writing them for five years or so," said the librarian. "We keep telling her she should collect them into a book, but she doesn't seem interested. Right now, they're just clippings pasted in a loose-leaf binder. We have a copy, of course." She leaned forward and confidentially breathed a mint-scented secret. "She isn't an official

94

historian, you know, not one of those stuffy ones with a bunch of letters after her name, but she's as good as any of them. Mostly, she interviewed old-timers and printed what they told her."

With that caveat disclosed, she brought the binder to Jason.

He sat in the reading room and skimmed the pages. The columns were a who-was-who and what-was-what of local history. One was about the old sawmill. Another told about the lumber baron who gave his name, and nothing else, to the park. A series of articles told about the Buckskins, their history, their early relations with the Sioux, French fur traders, and he almost turned the page before the word caught his eye —the windigo.

Hester had interviewed a psychologist who was studying the Indians and their customs and beliefs. One was about the windigo, a monster skeleton of ice that roamed the forest in the winter. The fearsome man-eater could be killed by various methods. Its heart of ice could be melted, but no instructions were included, not even pouring hot fat down the throat.

There were other windigos, or windigog, using the Indian plural. Algonquin Indians suffered from a psychosis that had been spread through the North Woods and up to Hudson's Bay. It was, as Charley Rogers had described it, a hunger madness that came in winter, when people believed they were possessed by the spirit of the ice monster. They saw their friends and family as succulent, tasty beavers. Jason almost smiled. He remembered the scene from *The Gold Rush*, where the hungry miner saw Charlie Chaplin as a large chicken.

But this was no comedy.

The afflicted people often begged to be killed. They sometimes committed suicide. If they weren't stopped, they might kill and eat members of their own families. Hester wrote that Windigo Pond was named for such an incident, but didn't mention Isaac Broadbow. There were cases in psychological and historical records, but none for years, probably because government assistance made sure the Indians weren't hungry enough to eat each other.

Yes, Virginia, Jason thought as he closed the binder, there is a windigo.

He stood, stretched, and glanced at his watch. Hours had passed, and it was time for supper. He left the library, crossed the street, and ate again at Muskyville. He thought of the date ahead, decided on less spicy food and had a ham supper. Afterward, he strolled the streets and, at seven, found Erica's address a few blocks from First Street, at a two-story, white clapboard house. The bottom floor was a craft shop. He looked in the bay window and saw, by light in what had probably been the kitchen, a display of knick-knacks, including ceramic dolls in Indian costumes, stuffed cloth loons, and aprons with embroidered ducks. No musky stuff, he noticed, as if women who shopped here didn't want to be reminded of fish. A window on a door on one side of the porch showed a flight of stairs going to the second floor. He pushed the doorbell and heard a faint buzz from inside. In a few seconds, Erica came down to open the door. She wore a light blue dress, with her blond hair in a pony tail. Jason marveled again at how sensible she seemed. She even wore flat shoes and her face had only a touch of make-up. They walked back to Peavey and down almost to the Chamber of Commerce building. The theater was so small, with such a tiny marquee, that he hadn't noticed it before.

She looked at the display poster and said, "I think it's a vampire movie, so it's fright night."

Not exactly. It was a comic spoof with Dracula's castle,

moved to America, and a girls' college softball team stranded there. The old vampire, a bumbling, officious oaf, had a descendant, teen-aged Desmond, who didn't want to be a vampire. He and Dracula kept popping out of closets and boxes and holes, and the audience cheerfully heckled every time they flapped their black cloaks and showed their fangs.

Jason felt like he was on a high school date, with popcorn and a goofy movie, holding hands during the scary parts, laughing together at the funny scenes and, after the movie, a quiet walk back to her place. It had been an entertaining evening, not a romantic one, and they kissed politely before she closed the door. He waited until a light came on upstairs, the curtain drawn back, and she waved at him. She was safe.

The simple movement reminded him that this wasn't the big city. He shouldn't have worried, not in a quiet town like Jackpine. He wasn't used to a place so safe and dull. Even the walls seemed boring without graffiti. It wouldn't be a bad place to spend the rest of his life, he decided. But what the hell would he do? He could live at the cabin, but that would be just running away from everything. Besides, he had to earn money. Sooner or later he'd probably return to Milwaukee, back on the force. Well, all decisions had to wait for answers about Unk Roland's death.

As he drove back to the cabin, he chuckled as he remembered what happened in the movie. Dracula turned himself into a cloud of dust and was sucked into a vacuum cleaner. If only all problems could be ended so conveniently, with the villains easily defeated.

The cabin was dark, as he'd left it, with no sign that anyone had visited or vandalized it. The hunting arrow still stuck in the door. Jason stopped the car, got out, and listened. There were no unusual sounds, so he searched the area, then unlocked the door and entered carefully. He thought he'd sure feel silly if somebody was there with Roland's gun. Everything looked the same as when he left. He made sure the gun was still in the drawer, then looked at his watch. It was almost eleven, but he didn't feel fatigue, only a slight nagging ache in his back. With no breeze from the lake, the air felt warm and stifling. He decided to buy a fan the next day. Even a small one would be better than nothing, although the generator would have to work over-time. He stretched out on the cot and decided he was tired after all. He fell asleep in a few minutes. The ice skeleton appeared again, in winter on Layton Avenue, with streets covered with a slippery sheen of ice. As the bouncing bullet chased Jason, the skeleton loped beside him, and their feet thumped loudly on the street.

He jerked awake, sitting upright on the cot as his heart hammered a ragged rhythm.

The thuds came from the cabin's west wall. Then he heard a howl, a weird ululation that reminded him of the dismal wail of jackals on moonlight nights on the African plains. He heard another thump against the side of the cabin. Damned Bearclaw, he swore silently. Probably shooting arrows again. Next came a bellow, this time more like a human imitating an elephant.

When the south window crashed and spit glass halfway across the room, Jason decided he'd had enough. He got out of bed, stepped around a rock on the floor, opened the drawer, and pulled out the Ruger. He ripped open a box of bullets, flipped out the loading gate, and jammed shells into the cylinder. Then he padded to the window and crouched down behind it as a loud scream came from the woods to the east. Somebody imitating a wildcat, he guessed. Outside, moonlight showed a slight movement under a pine tree. It had to be a human, and maybe only one, although others might be hiding nearby.

He knew he couldn't be seen if he stayed away from the window, so he stepped back, crouched, thumbed the hammer, aimed through the broken window, and shot high, about twenty feet above the ground and into the trees. He saw no movement, but heard noises in the brush, then silence. He sighed. He could go back to bed, but he wouldn't rest until he knew no one was out there.

He found a dark blanket to drape over his shoulders, gripped the revolver in his right hand with his index finger outside the trigger guard, and pulled the blanket around him with his left hand. He felt somewhat silly, like Desmond in the movie, wearing a blanket for a cape. He probably looked sillier than Desmond, but he didn't expect anyone to see him, especially with the blanket blending into the darkness. That shot probably would have scared off a bear.

He quietly opened the door on the lake side and slipped out. He flattened against the wall and slowly walked to the west, his feet testing each step before he put his weight down. He entered the woods where he'd seen the movement. As he expected, he found no trace of anyone. He returned to the cabin, put the gun on the floor beside the bed, and crawled back under the sheet. He heard the whine of mosquitoes coming through the broken window.

He'd scared off whoever had been in the trees. He hoped he'd scared off the ice skeleton and the bouncing bullet, too.

Memories of the strange dream nagged at him. He wondered if it came from somewhere in his subconscious memory. He felt as if the cabin had some sort of lingering spirit that affected him.

This time he dreamed that large, flapping, black bats pursued him through the woods. The creatures looked nothing like the comic Dracula or Desmond. Even as he dreamed,

Jason wondered, is this a new version of the windigo nightmare, and how long will it haunt me? Could he exorcise the nightmare, or this cabin, or his own possessed spirit, or would that damned ice skeleton hang around evermore like a croaking raven?

Chapter 14

The Thing with No Conscience

The nightmare was gone when Jason woke and looked at his watch. It was nine o'clock, with the summer's heat just beginning to hit. He tested his back carefully by stretching his arms out to the sides, then up, down, out again. As he swung his feet off the cot to the floor, he felt stiff in all the wrong places, like the Tin Man after a rain. He walked to the east window and looked out at the lake. Fishing boats were again silhouetted on water that glistened like sprinkled diamonds. One fisherman pulled in a small fish, shook his head sadly, worked out the hook, and tossed his catch back into the water.

Jason slipped on a shirt and pants over his briefs and then washed his face and hands. A breakfast of eggs and bacon made him ready to start the day. He pulled on socks and old high-top boots and laced them. In the years he'd prowled and played in the forest, he'd never seen a rattlesnake, but they were there, and the one day he didn't wear boots he might be snakebit. Besides, the boots kept sandburs, thorns, and ticks away from his legs.

He found the broom, swept up the rock and glass shards, then taped a page of the newspaper over the broken window.

As he walked into the forest, he plunged into a damp, greenish gloom, silent but for the soft twitter of birds, the rustle of his feet in brush, and the ubiquitous hum of mosqui-toes. He crossed back and forth, looking for any hint of who might have been there the night before. As he expected, he found no sign. Strolling in the forest wasn't exercise, so he began to stride, whipping his feet through the brush as he swung his arms. He moved south, parallel to the edge of the lake, within a few hundred feet of the shore, making sure he could glimpse patches of blue lake through the trees.

The shadowed forest seemed to hide unseen dangers, yet he and Bobby had played here when they were kids and never been afraid, not even of what the Buckskins called "the haunted rock." Neither he nor Bobby knew why the rock was supposed to be haunted. It was just something Bobby had heard from his parents, an old story they mentioned but never explained.

Now, as he walked briskly through the woods, the rock suddenly loomed ahead, large and greenish, like some weedy sea behemoth. He was surprised to find it so soon. But no, it hadn't moved closer to the cabin, he realized. When he was a kid, he was half as tall. The rock, like the lake drop-off, seemed farther away then. The rock wasn't as large as he remembered it. His difference in size accounted for that, too. But it was as wide as the cabin and at least twenty feet high, with a slanted flat surface on the west side.

As a kid, Jason wondered how such a large boulder got there, for it was alone, surrounded and shaded by the tall pines. Later, when he studied geology, he learned that the rock was an "erratic," carried there by one of the continental glaciers. On the north, buried under the grass and dirt and trees, the rock probably had left bedrock scratches where it had been pushed for miles by the creeping face of the ice.

Charley Rogers had once said the rock was thrown across the lake by Nanabazhoo, the giant warrior who became the basis for the Hiawatha poem.

A thin layer of scrawny greenish lichen grew on the rock. The stuff was edible. It had sometimes saved starving trappers or Indians. All you had to do, Charley said, was scrape it off and boil it into mush. The trouble was, it tasted so bad that it wasn't much better than starving.

Charley also talked about the *muzzinabikon,* the picture writing on the rock. The figures didn't seem like writing, but more like geometric designs of dull colors. When he was a child, Jason thought a giant must have painted them, for they were about ten feet above the ground. Now, seeing them again, Jason realized any adult wearing snowshoes and standing on a high snowdrift could easily have drawn the figures.

Jason stared up at them. What had seemed prehistoric graffiti now made more sense. A bumpy line with dots underneath suggested snow dropping from a cloud. He couldn't guess the meaning of the black circle, but inside it were two human stick figures with arms and legs outstretched. They also had wide, oval tails, and Jason realized with a shock that they must represent the children the mother thought were beavers. Underneath them were crosses, like stacked wood, and wavy lines that could mean fire. A much larger stick man had lines where the ribs would be. Jason thought it was probably a skeleton. On the other side of the circle were two figures. One was a woman, with breasts and a line sticking out from one of them. Was that the fish spear thrown by the other large stick figure?

So this is where it happened, he thought, and then corrected himself. No, this is where the story is told. Underneath the figures, he saw one more symbol. An arrow pointed toward the cabin.

That place seemed almost a lodestone for nightmares, danger, and death.

As he walked back, he reminded himself that he should lock up whenever he went outside. He hadn't considered it before. Fishermen were the only people who came to the area. They never seemed threatening, although one could easily beach his boat and steal stuff. Jason assumed they were honest enough to tamper only with the truth. But last night's visitor was no fisherman or practical joker. It had to be someone, maybe more than one, who knew about him and probably knew something of the windigo story. That could be anybody living in the area. After all, if Charley knew the story, then every other Indian probably did too, and maybe every anthropologist who'd stayed with them.

It was the sort of story Unk Roland would have used in one of his men's magazine articles. He'd claim it was folklore, but the editors would edit out the disclaimer to make the story more sensational. After that happened, Roland often said he had to explain to other anthropologists that he wasn't really crazy. Could he really have believed something like an ice-skeleton monster cannibal? No, although he'd say, "It's no more fantastic than a virgin birth." When he talked to scientists who were religious, he liked to tell them that religion was only an arrogant, selfish human wish to stay alive forever, even after death, "Just like vampires."

If Roland had joined the Zinners, why hadn't he said anything about it? Easy enough to guess. When somebody does something dumb, he doesn't want other people telling him how foolish he is. And, no doubt about it, Unk usually would have considered the Zinners a bunch of nuts, somewhere between snake-kissers and "Om" chanters.

Jason entered, stripped to his shorts, picked a towel from

the pile on the shelf in the corner and went out to the lake.

Unk always had been in his right mind. So the Zinners lied. He hadn't joined them. He grinned as he thought, Roland a Zinner? It's as believable as the Pope saying the Shroud of Turin was the burial cloth of Elvis.

Jason draped the towel over a bush and stuck a foot into the lake. The water was warm already. Under his toes, a few weeds writhed like skinny green snakes. He knew it would be clearer in deeper water, but it wasn't bad even this close to shore. He waded out until his toes felt the edge of the drop-off. Then he leaned forward and slowly swam out, turned, floated on his back, and watched the fishermen. They ignored him as long as he stayed out of casting distance. Good thing there aren't any water skiers, he thought. They'd likely run right over him before they saw him.

He thought he'd get the skull back in a few days; or would he? No, it might be turned over to a funeral home. Should there be a memorial service in Milwaukee, and maybe one up here?

When he decided he was clean and cool enough, he waded out, picked up the towel and walked to the cabin. Margaret Stuart, wearing her buckskin Indian outfit, nodded and crossed the grass as he approached. "Well, hello," he muttered, embarrassed. "How did you get here?"

"I walked. It isn't far, about two miles if you go around the bogs." She smiled. "I wouldn't mind if you didn't have anything on."

I'll bet, he thought.

"I just dropped by to say hello," she said. "Hope you don't mind."

"I can put on some coffee," he said. "Or is that against your religion?"

She shook her head. "We believe in eating natural

foods. Organic, you know. That includes coffee. If it comes from nature, it's our friend."

He thought, Like poison ivy?

She smiled brightly at him. "People say we're nature worshipers. And maybe we are. But we just follow our natural instincts."

"Good point," he said.

Good two points, he almost Freudian slipped as he tried to avoid staring at her blouse. Jason hadn't been with a woman for months, not since before he'd been wounded, but he'd been aroused enough to know he hadn't lost the urge. He just hadn't had a chance to indulge it. He felt it now, as he again thought of her display the other night.

"We're natural in other ways, too," she said, drawing closer to him. She slowly touched the buttons of her blouse, caressing them, slowly teasing them open. The blouse parted a few inches and he could see the cleavage behind it. Then she stepped forward, pulled the blouse off, and tossed it to the ground. She stood with her breasts nudging his bare chest. She reached down gently with one hand and whispered, "I hope you like the natural way as much as I do. But if you'd like it some other way, I can do that, too."

She tilted her face up and, as they kissed, her tongue squirmed quickly in his mouth.

He felt it was like swallowing a snake. He wondered why he was slightly repulsed. It was the kind of adolescent fantasy some guys have as long as they live.

"Let's do it now," she whispered. "I'm ready. And you are too. I can feel it."

He felt so ready he wasn't sure he could wait. But he didn't move.

She asked, "What's the matter? Is it against your religion? Don't worry about that.

She squeezed him gently and he tried not to moan.

"It doesn't care," she said. "Like the old saying, it doesn't have a conscience."

Maybe not, he thought, but this one has caution.

"You should join us, live with us," she whispered. "You'd love it. We all do. We do whatever we like."

"A lot of this?" he almost gasped.

"As much as we want, whenever we want to, with anybody we want to. Come back with me. You'll find out."

It reminded him of a pitch from a salvation salesman. No, very obviously a saleswoman. He stiffened the rest of his body. She felt it, sensed herself rejected, and drew away. "You don't want to," she said, her voice even. "That's all right. It's probably too much for you to understand now."

He wanted to say that maybe he understood enough, but he kept silent. Her breasts swung freely as she bent down to pick up her blouse.

"It's so hard to convince some people," she murmured. "But if you get to know us, you'll realize what we have to offer. The Wilderness of Zin is really a great thing. We'd do anything for it."

Maybe that's the trouble, he thought. She'd do anything.

"But you wanted to," she said as she buttoned the blouse. "I could tell."

"Do you want a ride back?"

She shook her head. "I made it here. I can make it back. But come over and see me some time."

It sounded like an innocent parody of the Mae West line.

As he watched her walk away and disappear into the forest, he sighed in relief. She hadn't made any accusations or recriminations. She'd accepted the rejection with almost religious fatalism, as if she'd expected it.

Jason decided that women were strange. And the biggest

mistake is to think they're all strange in the same way. A woman could be mad as hell if he made advances to her, and just as mad if he turned down her advances. But Margaret wasn't angry. Maybe she really wasn't that much interested in him. After all, he knew he wasn't some sort of irresistible superstud. Maybe she felt pity. Not because he didn't respond, but because he wasn't part of her true religion. Maybe the inquisitors felt the same way when they put the torch to the heretics.

He felt soiled by her touch, and went back to the lake for another swim.

Must be a hell of a belief system, he thought. The anything she'd do included sex. What else would she do for her religion?

Chapter 15

Just Above Diddly

Reading the newspaper, mild exercise, and loafing took up most of Jason's day. As he ate a spare supper of a corned beef sandwich, he wondered about his morning encounter with Margaret Stuart. Was he too suspicious of her? He decided to trust his instincts and assume she had some other motive than a yen for casual sex. As he swallowed the last bite of sandwich, he heard a motor outside. He looked out the west window and saw a sheriff's car parked beside his Honda.

Jack Mink climbed out and walked to the cabin just as Jason opened the door. The deputy stood casually, one hand on a hip, the other gesturing to the arrow stuck in the door. "Looks like open season around here."

Jason explained what had happened during the night, ending with, "I have an idea who was here, but no proof."

Mink asked, "You going to leave the arrow there?"

"Might as well," said Jason. "If Willard wants it, he can come get it. I don't even know for sure if it's his, so anybody wants it can have it."

"Maybe he isn't so anxious to come visiting," said Mink, grinning. "He might get stomped again."

"I didn't stomp him very hard. Besides, he's probably

on to that trick now."

Mink said, "Or maybe not. I don't think he's heap wise Injun. Maybe he figures an arrow isn't worth the trouble. But that isn't what I came for."

"Tell me over coffee, if you want some. Or maybe you'd like a beer." He looked at his watch. "It's after five. You should be off duty by now. I've spent the day goofing off here, so I could use some company."

"Sheriff wants to see you," said Mink.

"What the hell for? I'm under arrest or something? For stomping somebody's shin?"

"I'm not supposed to say. Not much, anyway. But you're not in any trouble."

"That's good."

He thought that Margaret hadn't acted as if she'd accuse him of rape or anything else. Apparently she hadn't, not if he could believe Mink. Could he? If he has orders to bring somebody in, it'd be easiest and safest to lie. Sheriff wants to see you. No problem. Just come down to the station for a few minutes. He wouldn't add, maybe spend the night in jail.

Jason asked, "If I'm not in trouble, who is?"

"Nobody." Mink again gestured to the arrow. "Well, you might be, but not from us. The sheriff wants to talk to you, that's all."

Jason knew one way to find out if Mink was really serious. "Could it wait?"

"No big hurry. You can even come in by yourself tomorrow if you want to. But it is something that concerns you and your uncle."

"Would the sheriff still be in by the time we get there?"

"He'll stay unless I call in and say you're not coming."

"He wants me to come in with you?"

"If you do, I'd bring you back here."

Jason was still suspicious. Since when was a deputy used as a taxi driver?

"Besides," Mink added, "the sheriff's wife died a few months ago."

"I'm sorry," said Jason.

"Well, you can bet he was, too. Fine woman, Mrs. Skinner. And it happened sudden. Her car hit a deer."

Jason hadn't seen that story in the paper. Apparently he hadn't read that far.

"So the sheriff, he spends a lot of time at the office. I think he hates to go home. Anyway, he asked me to bring you, if you'll come in."

"I'd rather take my own car," said Jason. "You say tomorrow morning's all right?"

"Fine," said Mink. He turned and stepped to the door of the squad car, and Jason followed. As the deputy started the engine and reached for the radio, Jason held up his hand. "Okay, I'll go with you."

Mink grinned. "Couldn't resist the curiosity?"

Jason grinned back. "Maybe I just want you to get some overtime bringing me back here."

"If I got overtime, I'd be retired by now."

"Give me a minute to make sure everything is all right inside. I'd better turn off the generator, too."

Mink nodded, shut off the engine, got out, and stood beside the car. A few minutes later Jason climbed into the passenger seat. As they drove away, Mink asked, "You don't lock your door?"

"Anybody can get in if he really wants to. Besides, I don't have hardly anything worth stealing."

"How about your gun?"

"The gun?"

"The twenty-two," said Mink. "We searched the cabin, remember?"

Jason shrugged. "That gun isn't worth much. Maybe a hundred bucks. I never thought about pricing it. If it's stolen, I've got the serial number. Unk Roland did, I mean. I saw it in his safety deposit box in Milwaukee."

As they drove to town, Mink used the radio to tell the sheriff about the events at the cabin. After that, the deputy and Jason talked randomly about the weather, fishing prospects, local tourist business, just time-filling chatter. Jason sensed that Mink didn't want to give out any details about why they would see the sheriff. Maybe the deputy had orders to keep quiet about that. After they parked in the lot at the sheriff's office, Mink got out, stretched, and waited for Jason. Then they entered the building. A thin, elderly deputy sat at Mink's usual desk and talked on the radio about who would be off for supper. Jason guessed the man as retired military or maybe from some city police force. He looked up at Mink and said, "Sheriff's waiting for you."

"He's always waiting for somebody," Mink grunted as he led the way into the next room. Skinner sat behind his desk, one foot propped on the edge of the waste basket as he stared out the window and puffed a long, thin cigar.

Mink said, "You're doing it again. You know you're not supposed to."

The sheriff stared at the cigar lovingly and put it back between his teeth. "You know, Jack," he grumbled, "I got so I don't care. This job, this cigar, they're about all I got left." He gestured to the captain's chair on the other side of the desk. "Sit down, Mr. Targo."

Jason sat and leaned back comfortably. "Might as well call me Jason, unless there's some reason to be formal. Is there?"

Skinner puffed the cigar again. "No. I'd like you to give

112

Jack a statement about that situation at the cabin, you shooting into the woods, and why. And I need you to make another statement on what happened on," he glanced at the file on his desk, "on Saturday? Damn, seems like a long time ago."

"Why another statement? What about?"

"About finding the remains of your uncle."

"I told you everything then."

The sheriff shrugged and spread his hands. "Well, you know how it is, you being in the business."

"Yeah, I know. That means you suspect me of something."

"Oh no, we don't suspect you at all." Skinner seemed uncomfortable. He shifted his position in the chair, stared again at the cigar, and avoided Jason's eyes. "We'd like you to go through it again, just in case you remember something you didn't put in before."

Jason thought, Or change my story? What the hell is going on? He rose and said, "Let's do it."

Skinner nodded. As Jason and Mink left the room, the sheriff put his feet on the desk and puffed smoke rings into the air.

Jason again told Mink what had happened during the night. The deputy handed the notes to a secretary to be typed, then stood, stretched, and said, "Glad that's over for now. I could use supper. You hungry?"

"I'd share a pizza."

Mink said, "Sounds good to me," just as Skinner walked out of his office and sat on the edge of the desk. "Something else, Mr. Targo," he said. "Give us some more information about your uncle."

"I know a lot. We could be here all week. What are you getting at?"

"Anything you know about who the professor might have been dealing with up here."

Jason stood up, ignoring Skinner's hand motioning for him to stay seated. "You can arrest me and I can call a lawyer. You show me a warrant or I'm walking. Or you can tell me what this is all about."

Skinner sighed. "We got a call from the crime lab in Madison this morning," he said. "They examined your uncle's skull. There were scratches on it."

"I saw those. It had a hole, too. Maybe made by some animal."

"The scratches were made," said Skinner, "probably by a bear. Anyway, the scratches aren't as important as the hole. It's an exit wound."

"Not from an animal?" Jason frowned in thought, then sat back down, stunned.

Mink said, "We assume the hole came from a large caliber bullet, from bone blowing out, not being bashed in. The bullet probably entered the right eye. There's a nick in the edge of the socket."

Skinner nodded again. "Looks that way. Mr. Targo, you think he might have done it himself?"

"I don't think so," said Jason, still trying to digest the new revelation. "I hadn't seen him for months before he disappeared, but I'd talked with him on the phone every two weeks or so. As far as I know, he felt fine. He didn't sound depressed."

"That's what I thought," said Skinner, quietly. "From the few times I talked with him, I never thought of him as somebody who'd do something like that. He seemed interested in what he was going to do."

Jason asked, "What do you mean? What was he going to do?"

"Well, I don't really know. I just got the impression, from his attitude, I guess, that he planned some projects for the future, maybe the next week, or even the next year. But actually, we usually just talked about fishing. He never said anything about hunting, not that I remember."

Jason said, "He didn't like to kill for the fun of it and he didn't need much meat."

Mink asked, "Did he have a big gun, like a hunting rifle?"

Jason shook his head. "And no big revolver either, not that I know of."

"It could have been a hunting accident. But you know we have to assume somebody could have shot him on purpose. Did he have any enemies?"

"Again, none that I know about. Nobody who'd want to shoot him, anyway."

"Okay, not on purpose, maybe," said Mink, "but somebody did shoot him."

"On purpose or not," Jason grated, "I want to know who did it."

Skinner nodded solemnly. "We do too, but you know how small the chances are of us finding anything."

Jason nodded. "Somewhere between piss-poor and diddly."

Skinner stared at his cigar and put it into an ash tray. "If we're lucky, maybe just above diddly. But don't get any ideas about doing something yourself. This is police business, but my police, not yours."

Jason nodded again. "Of course. I understand that. But if you learn anything, you'll tell me, won't you?" He remembered how Skinner had dodged the question the first time, so he wasn't surprised at the sheriff's answer.

Skinner stood, held out a hand and said, "If you think of anything, you let us know, all right? Let's keep in touch."

Jason shook hands and walked out into the early evening's still hot sunlight. Mink shook his head and smiled as they strolled toward an Italian restaurant on Peavey Street.

Jason asked, "What's the matter?"

"My dad told me about when the FBI came into the North Woods and tried to capture Dillinger. The only people got shot or killed were lawmen or innocent bystanders. The sheriff knows about that too, even if he's not old enough to remember it. So you can understand why he doesn't like you or any other outsiders sticking their noses in the law up here."

Jason smiled grimly. "The law up here? It reminds me of how some primitive people have a different idea about criminals."

"Don't tell me," said Mink, also grinning. "Instead of going to the law, us savages like to kill and scalp our enemies."

"According to the law, that's pretty savage. Nowadays, if somebody kills your uncle, it's none of your business. It's not even a crime against you. It's against the state, and it's the law's job to catch and punish the killer. And if the law can't do it, that's just tough shit for both you and your uncle."

"I see how you could feel that way," said Mink. "And I suppose you could also feel the sheriff is just a hick, old-fashioned law-dog."

Jason said, "Well, I feel like that old-fashioned law-dog just marked his territory by pissing on me."

Chapter 16

Where There's Smoke

As they drove back to the cabin, Mink said, "You aren't much help. I guess us hick flatfeets will have to solve this all by our lonesomes."

"Hey, if I knew who did it, I'd tell you," said Jason.

As Mink drove past the Wilderness of Zin, the sight of the sign seemed to nudge his curiosity. He asked, "You have any trouble with those people?"

"I wanted to ask you the same question."

"Mine first," said Mink.

"No, no real trouble." He didn't mention the earlier experience with Margaret. Besides, that couldn't be called trouble. "Why should I have any trouble?"

"The Zinners say your uncle joined them. Personally, I don't think so, but that's what they say. Some people claimed their relatives were brainwashed when they joined and signed over their property. A few heirs tried to contest the wills, but the Zinners got everything clear and legal. Most of those people were old folks, died of natural causes. And nobody could prove they were crazy."

Jason grinned and said, "Maybe they grabbed onto the Zinners' religion like a last hope, a life saver, maybe a soul saver. Some people get disillusioned with their religions.

Here they can get some sex and healthy food and a chance to be reincarnated as a rock instead of going to hell."

"Makes sense," said Mink, "although I don't know if any rocks say they're happier now."

Jason said, "I don't know if the Zinners would kill Uncle Roland to get his land. Maybe them telling me I should give it to them is just a bluff. The lawyer in Milwaukee has Roland's will. If there's a new one, nobody told me. Besides, seems to me Lestray would have told everybody if the Zinners were in the will. Instead, he's telling me I should give the land to them. All they did was try to get me to join them, but that's natural. Most religions try that."

Mink nodded. "They do. With our religion, though, the Indian one, we don't try to convert people. The Zinners copied a lot of our religion, or what they think it is, but they added the evangelical angle."

"I think they copied from everybody," said Jason.

Mink shrugged. "As long as they leave us alone. Sometimes they don't. You saw that when you tangled with them and Willard at the mall."

"I guess they don't all do missionary work, though. I think everybody does pretty much what he wants to."

"So I hear," said Mink. "And they share everything. And from what I also heard, I mean really everything!"

Jason grinned. "I should think they'd be up to their asses in babies and clap, but they might be sensible about things like that. And from what I've seen, there isn't much else to share."

"Yeah. They live in teepees, for Christ's sake! Or for Gitchee Manitou's sake, which is just as dumb. I mean, we lived in teepees and brush huts for maybe a thousand years, but that was because we didn't have plank walls and floors and insulation. If they do a lot of screwing in the winter, maybe it's the only way to keep warm."

They drove along the narrow road through trees in deep shadow from the setting sun.

"Sorry to cause you all this trouble," said Jason.

"If I didn't expect trouble, I wouldn't have this job. Besides, this isn't exactly trouble, just a little extra work."

"You're probably too polite to say it's a pain in the ass, and now you'll have to go back to town."

"Why?" Mink seemed puzzled for a second. "Oh no, I keep the car. I have so much work out here, with all this private land near the reservation, I'm on call all the time. This is practically my own car."

Jason said, "It's about eight. You must have been on duty for a long time."

"About eleven hours now. Sometimes I think that because the sheriff doesn't want to go home he wants company day and night. I've told him that, too. I was kidding, naturally. Maybe."

They drove into the clearing and Mink parked the car. Jason stared out the windshield and studied the front of the cabin. No one seemed to be at the cabin. The door was still closed, and he didn't see any other broken windows. Then he tensed in the seat, and stuck his head out the window. "Listen."

"I don't hear anything," said Mink. "Just the generator."

"Yeah, and I turned it off," Jason said quietly.

As they climbed out of the car, he saw a wisp of brownish smoke curl from the south side of the cabin, perhaps out of the broken window. Mink pulled out his revolver and held it pointed into the air as they stepped toward the cabin.

Mink muttered, "There's smoke, but I don't see any fire."

Jason watched the building carefully, looking for any movement, while the Indian moved his eyes from side to side, watching for anyone in the area.

Jason walked to the north side, peeked around the corner of the cabin, duckwalked to the window, shaded his eyes, and peered inside.

"Holy shit! Get back," he shouted. He ran around to the door, jerked it open, and stopped at the threshold to stare at the stove. The burner glowed brightly under a pan of oil. A haze of dark smoke rose to layer the ceiling and flow out around the edge of the newspaper over the broken window. Jason stepped inside quickly, grabbed a towel, covered his hand as he turned off the burner, then quickstepped across the room to open the door on the other side.

Mink stood in the doorway and watched. "Pretty soon that would have spattered into the burner and caught fire," he muttered. "I don't suppose you left it on."

"Even if I'd left the stove on, you saw me turn off the generator. And I came back in here before we left to make sure everything was off."

"Well, I figured it wasn't you," said Mink quietly. "The body wasn't here then."

Jason's head jerked around as he stared blankly at the deputy. "Body?"

"The one out there under the trees," said Mink. "I haven't looked at it carefully, but he must be dead. His guts are hanging out."

Chapter 17

Cat and Mouse

Mink pointed toward a body in the grass under the trees to the south. It seemed like a bundle of clothing in a puddle of dark paint. They walked closer until Jason almost gagged on the stench of bile, blood, and excrement that hovered like a fog above the body. He told himself not to look at it, to look somewhere else and maybe he could keep his stomach down. No matter how many times he'd encountered this sort of scene, he'd always hated it.

Mink squatted, ignored the smell and flies and calmly put one hand on its neck. Jason thought Mink must be playing stoic Indian, or maybe he really was.

"I'd say it happened not very long ago," said the deputy. "Body's not that cool." He gently wiggled one of the fingers. "Rigor mortis hasn't even started in the extremities."

Jason thought Mink sounded like he was reciting from a textbook. Maybe it was the old cop game of being tough, avoiding any emotion that might seem to be a sign of weakness.

Jason forced himself to glance quickly at the face. It was unrecognizable, contorted in fear, hate, or maybe pain, with lips curled back in a feral grin. It seemed unnaturally pale, but that could be caused by lack of blood.

A yellow shirt was pulled up around the neck. The chest

had a great gash where red flesh showed like a side of beef in a butcher shop cooler. Below it, the stomach was slashed from side to side and the intestines spilled out on the grass. They were almost covered by black, buzzing flies. The body's hands clutched the guts, as if trying to stuff them back inside or ease the pain.

Mink rose, walked to the cruiser, got in, and Jason saw him speak into the radio mike. He came back and said, "Sheriff's coming out." Then he squatted by the body again. "You want to see what you can find? No touching, naturally."

"Oh, too bad! There's nothing gives me a bigger thrill than pawing around in somebody's guts. Maybe he swallowed a clue, and we could look for it inside him."

He turned and walked away to search the area, making sure he stepped on nothing that looked like evidence. He wondered if the killer could be watching from the woods.

"Speaking of clues, I've got one, maybe," Jason said. "The arrow that Bearclaw stuck in the door, it's gone. Maybe he came to get it and killed this guy."

"Maybe he came for the arrow, but we can be sure that Bearclaw didn't kill this guy. This is Bearclaw."

Surprised, Jason stepped back. "It is?"

Mink stood up again. "Can't hardly blame you for not recognizing him. You see that arrow anywhere?"

Jason shook his head. "I didn't notice it. I could look in the house."

"Don't bother."

"Yeah," said Jason, grinning. "I forgot. It's a crime scene, and us civilians have to keep out."

"You're still a cop," grunted Mink. "Maybe you don't have jurisdiction, but you can keep your eyes open and your brain working, can't you?"

"Yeah, but I don't know how to work this side of it. I've

never been an innocent bystander before."

"You're probably lucky if that's all you are."

Jason remembered the cop mentality from the streets. When something like this happens, you're a cop, a victim, a subject or a perp. "Perp," he muttered to himself.

"Huh?"

"Perpetrator. I never realized how childish that sounds. Like giving a killer a comic name to take away his personality. He's playing robber, and we're playing cops. The person who's killed isn't a human being. He's a victim. The person who did it isn't somebody with emotions or problems, just a perp. The witnesses and innocent bystanders are subjects. Now it seems like I was part of a little boys' secret club with our own rules and passwords."

"How does it feel to be a subject?"

"Like I don't belong to the club any more. Like maybe I'm accused of being in the wrong place or not paying attention. Maybe I committed a crime only Kafka could think up."

"Well, just for the record, you aren't accused of anything right now." They carefully, cautiously, walked around the clearing and cabin, but found nothing unusual, so they went back to the cruiser to wait.

A half hour later, almost at dusk, Skinner arrived. He climbed out of the car and approached them slowly, looking from side to side. The elderly deputy got out of the car and reached into the back seat to haul out the evidence kit and camera equipment.

"Sorry to have to see you again so soon," the sheriff muttered, then turned to Mink. "Bearclaw, huh? Where is he?"

Mink pointed.

Skinner peered into the dimness under the trees. "Just enough light left to see. There's something about a pan of oil on the stove? Somebody trying to burn you out?"

"I guess so," said Jason. "Would have done it, too, if we hadn't come back in time."

"Yeah, if," grunted Skinner. "But it worked out all right. You two can go into the cabin, see if there's something out of place."

"We'll check out the gun, too," said Mink.

Jason asked, "What the hell for?"

"To make sure it's still there or if it's been fired. When the doc gets through digging into that body, he might find a bullet."

"Hell," Jason exclaimed, "you know I didn't do it!"

"Oh, sure, but if that gun's missing, we want to try to find it. After all, we can be pretty sure the guy who was inside your cabin is the one killed Bearclaw."

They paused when they heard a siren's warble. It came from an ambulance, a blob of white moving through the dark trees as it slowly approached. As the sound of the siren died, Jason heard the sheriff mumble something about "Damned hot-rodders."

A Jeep followed and parked behind the ambulance. A short, middle-aged man climbed out. He wore a business suit and carried a black satchel. Jason didn't know him, but didn't need to guess who he was.

Two white-suited attendants emerged from the ambulance and leaned against it as they calmly waited.

The doctor shouted in the sudden silence. "Why the hell did you need the siren? You wanna make sure the bears know you're coming?" He turned to Skinner. "Let's get it over with. I got to get back to a Lion's Club meeting. I'm tail-twister. Where's the corpus delicious?"

Skinner put on a Queen Victoria expression as he pointed to the body. "We ain't amused by your humor. There's a man dead here."

"If he don't like my jokes, then he better speak up." He looked down at the body. "You got something to say, Mr. Bearclaw? No? I thought not." He squatted and stared at the body. "My official decision, he sure as hell looks dead to me. I suppose I gotta do the usual, though." He put a hand on the body's neck for a second. "Just like I thought, deader'n the proverbial doornail."

He stood, grunting uncomfortably, smiled as if happy at his choice of medical jargon and said, "Can I go back now?"

Jason thought that things were informal here. Or maybe the doc wasn't an official coroner. There was no mention of an inquest. And where would they find the people for one? Even the bears would have been scared off.

Skinner didn't bother to answer the doctor, just waved him away and muttered something about a "Damned tail-twister."

Mink whispered, "The sheriff and Doc Sanders don't get along too well."

"I could guess," said Jason, grinning.

Mink added, "Doc's all right, as a doc. Sheriff just doesn't appreciate his bedside manner. Trouble is, the doc doesn't like sick people, especially the ones who take all the pills and then die. Must be a terrible disappointment to him."

The doctor backed the Jeep carefully up the road. One of the ambulance attendants lit a cigarette.

"Yeah, smoke if you got 'em," said Skinner, "but you put the butts in the ash tray in your ambulance, got it?"

"Aw, shit," grumbled the smoker. "You think we're stupid?"

Skinner answered with, "We find a butt around here, it's evidence. If it has your fingerprints on it, then maybe you're a suspect. How'd you like that?"

The attendant took no chances. He climbed back into the ambulance to smoke.

"Let's get to work," said Mink, and turned toward the cabin. Just before they entered, Jason looked back and saw Skinner kneeling beside Bearclaw's body. The elderly deputy was loading film into a twin-lens reflex camera.

Jason stopped at the door and looked inside, studying the room, searching for something out of place. The only unusual thing he saw was the pan of oil.

Mink asked, "That's regular cooking oil in there?"

"I assume so. I had almost a full bottle of it." He looked inside the pan. "Looks like some water in the bottom. That'd make it spatter more when it boiled."

Mink walked in and looked at the stove. "We'll go over this for prints, naturally. You probably got yours on the knob when you turned it off."

"I used a towel," said Jason. "If there were prints, I probably wiped them off."

"We'll check the pot handle, too. You know the routine, and you know we probably won't find anything useful. Let's check on the gun."

Jason pointed to the dresser. "In the top drawer."

Mink took a jackknife from a pocket and used its bottle opener to hook the handle to pull out the drawer. Jason reached in, felt the layer of underwear and shook his head. "It's gone."

"You have the serial number, you said?"

"I suppose I can get it tomorrow from his safe deposit box in Milwaukee. I'll have to go there to make arrangements for his cremation."

Mink turned around slowly and looked at the room. "You see anything wrong?"

Jason turned and was startled to see Skinner leaning

against the doorway, watching. Jason said, "Something wrong? No, everything looks normal, even if we know he took the gun. I think we can assume he knew where it was. I'd also assume it was a man."

Skinner nodded. "You're right. A woman could do it. It's hard for me to believe that a woman would do something like this, though, even if it doesn't take much strength to cut somebody open like that." He looked around the room. "I think he didn't have to tear things up to find the gun because he knew where to look. But we don't know why he took it. Anyway, he knew you weren't here, but he probably didn't know where you went. I mean, your car was here. He wouldn't try to frame you if he knew you were with us, but he might of thought you were off in the woods someplace."

"I confess," said Jason, grinning. "I did it. Now it's up to you to prove how I did it when I was with you or Jack all the time."

"Very funny," Skinner grunted. "Damn good thing you were with us, or I'd be asking some serious questions. Remember, you and Bearclaw weren't exactly friends."

"There's a problem," Mink mused. "If the killer was trying to blame Jason, why would he try to torch the cabin?"

"Why ask me?" said Skinner. "And don't ask me why somebody left Bearclaw here, like a cat bringing home a dead mouse to show it off. This don't make sense, and it probably won't until we find out who did it."

Chapter 18

Bad News

The sheriff's car's headlights bored a tunnel between the pines as Skinner drove away from the cabin.

"I'm not looking forward to this," said Skinner. He chewed on his cigar thoughtfully, then muttered a quiet, "Shit." Obviously, he'd planned to spit out the window, but a heavy drizzle that began at sunset now pelted against the car window.

He cranked it down a few inches, spat quickly, then added another "Shit" when he saw brown liquid drip down the inside of the glass as he rolled it back up. "Makes me want to give up smokin'," he muttered. He drove through the rain for a few more minutes, then continued, "I've known the Wallers for years."

"Wallers?" asked the mystified Jason.

"Bearclaw's real name. He thought it was too Paleface, so he picked his new Indian one. His folks never liked what he was doin', with his fightin' and other trouble he was gettin' into. What he was doin' might be considered idealistic, or stupid."

Jason said, "Maybe somebody more idealistic or stupid killed him."

The sheriff took the cigar from his mouth, looked at it distastefully, and again rolled the window down a few inches. This time, he threw the stogie out. "That's it. If I'm not smoking them, I'm not hooked, am I? I can quit right now."

Jason grinned. "Until you light up the next one. It's fine with me if you quit right now. Somebody chewing on a cigar always reminds me of a monkey licking a dog turd."

Skinner grimaced. "Thanks. If I keep thinking of that, maybe I will quit. How come that remark about somebody being more militant than Willard? You think it was one of his pals did it?"

"Just speculation."

"I hope you're speculating something useful," Skinner said. "Otherwise, I could of left you back at the cabin."

"This wasn't my idea anyway," Jason muttered.

"I know, but I was hoping you'd be some help, you being a big city cop and all that."

Jason didn't bother to answer. Whatever the reason, he was glad to be riding with the sheriff on this trip. He didn't like the idea of somebody murdered on his property, and he wanted answers as much as Skinner.

"So what about being more militant?" the sheriff asked.

"I suppose you've already thought about one of his friends killing him. It happens all the time. When somebody is killed you look at the spouse first, then the family, then his friends."

"Yeah, some friendship. Like they say, who needs enemies?"

Jason shrugged. "You know what I mean. They argue, they drink, they get into fights, they kill each other."

"That looked like a hell of a lot more than just a fight."

"From what I saw the night they were at the cabin, it was like a power thing," said Jason thoughtfully. "Bobby didn't claim to be their leader, but the rest treated him like he was. Except Willard. For all I know, he might have killed me with that bow and arrow if it hadn't been for Bobby. He tried to calm everybody down at the mall, too. Of course, I'm not saying he would have killed Willard. It doesn't make sense that he'd turn on one of his followers. After all, he knew Willard a lot better than he knew me. That was years ago."

"Murder often doesn't make sense," said Skinner. "It may not make sense to us, but it did to the killer."

"We could come up with a dozen different ideas, but it'd be like arguing whether the moon is made of green or blue cheese. There probably wasn't any fight because somebody got hold of Uncle Roland's gun. People don't usually argue with somebody who has a gun. But it happens. And somebody could have shot Willard. And then, hell, I don't know what would make him gut Willard. Must have been some reason, though."

"Crazy person doesn't need a reason," said Skinner.

"You know better than that, Sheriff," said Jason. "A crazy person always has a reason. We may even understand it, but we don't agree with it. When we find the reason, maybe we can find who did it."

Skinner squinted through the windshield at the smudged tail lights of Mink's car. Mink drove slowly in the rain, trying to avoid animals and, like Skinner, trying to see the road in the downpour. "Nights like this make me sort of sad, like the whole world's goin' down the drain. Glad Mink's finally getting home. It's been a long day for him. Well, maybe we can get through with this part soon. I appreciate any help you can give me, even if you're not involved in this. It ain't in your jurisdiction."

"Oh my, ain't you the legal one," Jason said sarcastically. "My uncle was killed. Somebody else was killed on my land. I know, his land, but it's my land now, no matter what anybody else says. Somebody tries to burn down my cabin. You told

130

me before it was none of my business. Now you drag me into the rain to listen to you interrogate some suspects."

"I just thought I could use your help."

"Well, damn it, you don't have to sell me on the idea. I don't have anything else to do here except try to find out who killed my uncle and tried to burn down the cabin. That satisfy you? Far as I'm concerned, Willard got killed on my land and that makes it my case, even if I don't give a shit who killed him."

"I guess I came around this wrong," said Skinner quietly.

"You did if you want to get my vote," said Jason. "You didn't act like a sheriff. You acted more like an arrogant big city cop. Like I'm supposed to act, right?"

"Well, I'd appreciate any help you could give me."

"Well, I'll do it. And maybe I'll even vote for you some day."

The rain had slacked to a dismal drizzle when the two sheriff's cars stopped at the end of a mud-slick road. Mink parked in front of a small white clapboard house with a shingled front porch that dripped rain on brown painted steps. There was a light behind a curtained window, but someone saw or heard something, and the light beside the front door flicked on. The curtain flipped aside, someone peeked out, and the curtain slid shut again.

Jason looked at his watch. A little after eleven.

Mink got out of his car, slammed the door, and walked across the wet grass. As he got to the house, the door opened and a figure appeared inside. After a few seconds of talk, Mink turned and gestured for the others to come.

"Well, can't duck the job," said Skinner quietly as he got out of the car.

He can't, Jason thought, but knew he could duck it himself. This wasn't his job, and he didn't see how he could help.

But hell, he decided, if he was going to be in it, he'd go in all the way. He climbed out and looked into the sky. Rain dripped into his eyes. He couldn't see stars, or even sky behind the trees. The rain, he decided, might continue for days. He nodded to an Indian woman as he and Skinner entered. Jason guessed her age at about fifty, but she could also be forty or seventy. Her face was lined, seamed like dry, cracked mud. She wore jeans and a plain blue blouse of some light cloth. Her black hair was tied back in a braid. Beyond her, a man sat at a table in the middle of the living room. He stared at a jigsaw puzzle, or perhaps he stared past it at some hidden demon he alone could see. His face was set in a grim grimace.

"Come in," said the woman, quietly. "We've been expecting you."

Skinner and Jason looked at each other in silent questions.

The woman said, "If not tonight, then some other time. I suppose it's about Willard."

Skinner took off his hat, held it in front of him, and said, "I'm sorry, but I have some bad news."

"He's dead," said the man at the table.

The sheriff nodded. "How did you know?"

The woman said, "Whenever he was in trouble before, only one of you came to tell us. Now there are three."

"This is Jason Targo," said Mink.

The man at the table rose, came to them, and held out his hand. "Henry Waller," he said and, gesturing toward the woman, "Irma."

"Glad to meet you," said Jason as he shook hands. He didn't know if he should say anything else.

Mink said, "Professor Targo's nephew."

Henry nodded. "I know."

Irma asked, "What happened?"

132

She glanced at Jason, obviously wondering why he was there. He turned his head slightly to look at the interior of the house. It had flowered wallpaper on the walls, and the usual furniture scattered around. It was clean and worn, but not worn out. A few pictures, mostly scenic prints, hung on the walls. Skinner told the Wallers what had happened, leaving out the gruesome details, just telling how Willard had been found dead at the cabin. Henry glanced quickly at Jason. He apparently assumed that Jason hadn't done it or he wouldn't be there.

Irma asked, "Who did it?"

"We don't know yet," said Mink. "Mr. Targo and I were in town when it happened. We don't know of any witnesses."

Irma said, "I'll make coffee, if anybody wants some."

"I would, thanks," said Mink, as if he hoped it might keep her mind off what had happened, as if anything could do that.

She walked quickly through a door to the kitchen, and Jason heard a noise like a muffled sob.

Mink asked, "Do you know of anybody who might want to kill him?"

Henry avoided looking at Jason as he shook his head. "You know as much as I do," he said quietly. "After he started running around with Bobby Whitefish and that bunch, he stopped telling us anything important."

"Did he still live here?" asked Skinner.

"Sometimes. When he wasn't here, we didn't know where he was."

"I'll help with the coffee, Irma," Mink loudly said as he moved toward the kitchen, making no attempt to be quiet. Jason assumed the deputy wanted to talk to her about the same things Skinner wanted to know.

Henry said, "When he came here, sometimes he'd be in trouble and he wanted to hide out. Or he'd be drunk. Some-

133

times he wanted to argue, but he didn't come here just to do that."

Skinner asked, "Did he like to fight?"

"It was his temper," said Henry, nodding. "Once when he was drunk he wanted to fight with me. We were in the kitchen, and I hit him alongside the head with a hot spider. After that he never bothered me, and he didn't come here when he was drunk."

"When did that happen? When you hit him."

"I'd say a year ago, more or less."

"When's the last time you saw him?"

"Yesterday," Waller answered. "He was here about noon. He ate lunch and wanted to see if there was any mail for him. This was still his mailing address. He borrowed some car tools. You know, a spark plug wrench, things like that. I don't suppose any of this matters, does it?"

Skinner shrugged. "I don't know, Henry. But I needed to know anyway. It might mean something, but not yet. Did he say anything about where he was going, what he would do?"

Waller shook his head. "He didn't even say where he would fix the car, or if it was his car he would work on. I didn't pay much attention. Irma and I, well, we got sort of tired of listening to him complain, usually about what the Whites had done to our people. As if the Whites made him drop out of school. Did they make him get drunk, get into fights? He seemed to think they were all out to get him and his friends."

He looked at Skinner, his face suddenly drawn and more lined, his eyes glistening. "We had troubles when we were kids. We had some fights. Some of us hated the Whites, but we didn't do these kinds of stupid things to get ourselves killed. What's happening to these kids?"

Skinner shook his head. "I don't know."

Henry turned to stare at the jigsaw puzzle. It was a seascape, with most of the blue sky and clouds filled in. White sails showed on the bottom of the sky.

Jason saw that the pictures on the wall were also jigsaw puzzles, mounted and framed. He recognized a canal in Venice, and a mountain scene, probably Yosemite, with a round mountain split in half, with a narrow waterfall dropping to the bottom. He didn't see a TV set. It could be in another room, or maybe there was no reception this far from a station. Did the Wallers find escape in putting together jigsaw puzzles, looking at them and imagining?

Skinner said, "I grew up in a small town in Southern Minnesota. No Indians there, no Blacks, no Jews. And you know us kids still had fights between Irish and Polacks, things like that. But no, it wasn't as bad as what kids here have now."

"It wasn't this bad when I was growing up here," said Jason.

"That's right," said Henry. "You were a friend of Billy Dixon, before he called himself Whitefish. Now some of the Whites don't know if they can trust any of our young men."

"It's a shame," said Skinner. "And we hardly ever see the Buckskins in town."

"There's no need to go," said Henry. "Not any more, anyway. We have our own shopping center, and some of us feel we don't have to give the Whites our business. And sometimes we think they don't want us in town."

Skinner said, "One of these days you'll probably open a bingo parlor and end up taking all our money."

Henry almost smiled. "We're working on that. I guess it's a different version of Montezuma's Revenge."

Jason felt relieved. This was almost like a break in the sorrow Henry must be feeling. He hoped things were going all right with Mink and Irma in the kitchen, but hell, how could anything go all right at a time like this?

Unless the Wallers were hiding something or might remember something later, nothing could be learned here. Skinner seemed to agree with Jason's thoughts. The sheriff put his right hand on Henry's shoulder, a quick, almost embarrassed gesture, and then put his hat back on.

"We'll be going," he said. "Is there anything we can do?"

Henry shook his head. "What do we do about the body?"

"It has to go to Ashland," said Skinner. "You'll be notified when," and his voice trailed off.

"When you're done with it, after it's been chopped up and the pieces taken apart, then we can put what's left of him in his spirit house and hold our ceremonies to honor him and remember what he did that was good. I remember a few of the things and, shit, Sheriff, I'm sorry."

"We're all sorry," said Skinner, quietly.

"I know it has to be done."

"It'll help us find out who did it."

Mink entered from the kitchen. He sipped a cup of coffee, then quickly pointed his chin in the direction of the door. It seemed to be a mute routine. The sheriff raised his eyebrows in a small question, and the deputy answered with a barely perceptible shake of his head.

Henry said, "Have you talked to his friends?"

"No, not yet," said Skinner. "You're the first ones we've talked to. Maybe they were with him at the cabin. They were before."

"I heard about that," said Henry, nodding. "It was a bad thing they did, breaking the window. And I don't blame you, Mr. Targo, for shooting."

"I shot into the air," said Jason.

"And they ran, because they hadn't expected any opposition from you. They wanted you to run. I don't think they really want that land. They know it's cursed, but they're like dogs in the manger. They don't want it, but they don't want anybody else to have it either."

As if trying to avoid the subject, he moved to the table, sat, picked up a piece of the puzzle and stared at it.

Mink finished the coffee in one long gulp and put the cup down. "Anything you want, just give us a call," he told Henry.

Jason said, "I'm sorry this happened."

Waller nodded. "I'm sure you are, but you're not to blame. Maybe none of us are, not even the one who did it. Nothing is anybody's fault these days." He rose slowly from the chair and took a few steps toward the kitchen. "But even in the Garden of Eden, the snake was to blame. Ever since then it's always been somebody else's fault."

"Good-night, Henry," said Skinner. He put on his hat, turned toward the door, and added, "We'll let you know as soon as we find out anything."

He opened the door, and he and Mink walked out. As Jason closed the door, he caught a last glimpse of Henry shuffling toward the kitchen. He seemed twenty years older.

Mink said, "I didn't learn a thing from Irma. Okay if I go home and get some rest?"

Skinner nodded. "Do that. Been a long day for you."

Mink touched the brim of his hat and went to his car.

"I'll get you to a motel in town," said Skinner. "It's on the county."

"You'll have to arrest a couple of flat-land tourists to pay for it," said Jason, grinning.

"Just one. We don't have any fancy hotels here."

"I'd rather go back to the cabin."

"I want you safe in town. My deputy will take care of your place. Anybody tries to burn it down again is likely to get shot. And if anybody does any shootin', I want it to be one of my people."

Chapter 19

No Comment

On the way back to the cabin, Skinner used his cellular phone to make arrangements for a motel room for Jason.

"Like I said, we don't have any high class hotels here, but the Musky Manor ain't no Bates Motel, either." Skinner's solemn face contradicted any humor he might have suggested. "The place is clean. Doesn't give us any trouble. No loud parties, no hookers. Not that we have many up here anyway. I guess sex can't compete with fish. Bar and restaurant there, Musky Lounge, will give you something to eat if you need it."

Jason shook his head. The memory of Willard's body had removed his appetite. He decided a drink might help. He didn't need one to relax him physically. He needed to shut down his mind long enough for a night's rest.

"You'll be all right there," said Skinner. "We won't tell anybody where you are. Not that anybody will be interested. Nobody in town knows anything about Willard yet, I hope."

The deputy at the cabin was a lean, almost cadaverous young man. "Brian Schwartz," said the deputy as he extended his hand. "It sounds Irish and German. It's not, really. No Irish in me, and the Kraut was way back."

"Can it!" said Skinner. "You aren't running for sheriff,

139

not yet, anyway. Find anything important here?"

"Nothing. We'd have called you if we had."

"You ready to stay here tonight?"

Schwartz nodded. "I figure I'll spend some of the time in the car, the rest prowling around. It'll be pretty quiet. Nobody'll come close if they see the cruiser. Erica Chamberlain was out here."

"What?" This came as an explosion from Skinner.

Schwartz grinned, a lopsided, friendly grimace that reminded Jason of a young Tony Perkins. He wondered if he had *Psycho* on his mind? Not surprising, after what happened.

Schwartz said, "I let her take a few pictures."

Skinner asked, "Of the body?"

Schwartz shrugged. "Sure. It was covered, and I didn't let her get close to it. Made sure she didn't tromp around too much. Wouldn't let her in the cabin. No need to anyway. Nothing there she'd be interested in. She said she'd come out some other time for a picture of the cabin. I guess she meant in the daytime."

"She say who told her about this?"

Schwartz thought while he took a plastic package from a pocket. He opened it, stuck his fingers in, pulled out shredded stuff and tucked it into his mouth. Jason thought, Shit! Just what he needed. A chewer in the cabin. Then he realized the Tony Perkins clone was chewing bubble gum.

"Now that Ah thunk about it, Shurf," said Schwartz, grinning slyly, "seems to me that Miz Chamberlain didn't know anything that hadn't been said on the radio."

"So she's got a scanner," said Skinner. "Wouldn't be surprised. Well, hell, no big deal. She'd find out anyway."

"Maybe it's too late to get something into this week's paper," said Jason.

Skinner shook his head. "She'll make room for it. But

she'll check with me first, make sure she's not going off half-cocked with something we don't want her to print. She's sensible about it."

He took a cigar from a pocket and gestured with his other hand toward the cabin.

"Best be gettin' something to take with you and I'll drive you to the motel."

"I'd rather take my own car."

Skinner nodded as he lit his cigar. "Really best if you would," he grunted. "You can come back out tomorrow, whenever you're ready. Maybe in the afternoon after my people are done snooping around."

Jason went into the cabin and put a change of clothing into a grocery bag. As he went back outside, Skinner said, "I fixed it for you to get supper and drinks on the county if you want them." He grinned around his cigar. *Bon apetit.*"

From the looks of the inside of Jason's car, the deputies had already searched it. If they'd found anything, they hadn't told him. He drove to the Musky Manor on the highway west of town. The one-story brick, L-shaped building with a tiled roof looked out of place, almost a California mission style in an area where log cabins were more appropriate. He thought perhaps that was why it was that style. There were plenty of log cabin resorts in the area. Tourists come from all over, even California, and maybe they'd want something familiar.

The motel office was closed, with a "No Vacancy" sign lit outside. The Musky Lounge had more of a local theme, with knotty pine paneling, stuffed game heads on the walls, and a shell of a snapping turtle about two feet long. Its head was mounted beside the shell, with jaws large enough to sever a small wrist. A set of deer antlers on the wall was decorated with baseball caps from other parts of the country.

The pot-bellied bartender and a few customers stared listlessly at a TV. Jason asked the barkeep if the motel was really full.

The man turned and studied Jason. "You're Targo?"

Jason nodded.

"You must be the professor's nephew," said the bartender. "Pleased to meet you." He held out a damp hand and they shook. "Heard you were back," he continued. "Never met your uncle, understand. Seen him, but mostly just heard about him. He was like local color, ya know. Not exactly a tourist attraction, just somebody we liked to talk about. It must of been exciting going with him to all those strange places. I never get to go much. Tied down here, ya know. Terrible about your uncle. Like losing an old friend, ya know. Well, we got you in unit eight. Can't miss it. It's right next to seven, over in the corner. Hope it's okay. It really is all we got open, and we held it for you like the sheriff wanted."

He slid a key on a flat plastic disk across the bar. Jason took it and decided if he wanted a drink, he'd sit at a table far from the bar and pretend to be busy.

Unit eight had hunting pictures on the knotty pine walls. The furniture was unmatched, but clean and sound. The air conditioner hummed and the room felt cool and comfortable. He put the bag on the dresser and spread out the clothing. He decided to have a shower, then bed. But should he have a drink and supper first?

He twitched in surprise at the light knock on the door. When he pulled aside the curtain an inch and peered through the window, he saw Erica Chamberlain standing by the door, her hand raised to knock again. He opened the door and she smiled brightly. "Hi. Mind if we talk?"

He gestured toward the inside. She nodded and entered. "How'd you know I was here?" he asked as he closed the door.

She smiled again, showing more energy than expected for this time of the night.

"Let's say a little bird told me."

Jason grinned. "A little bird on a radio?"

She smiled back at him. "Hester Meldon. I don't know how she finds out, but she knows all, sees all, tells me, even at night."

"I thought you'd be busy now. Don't you have a paper to put out?"

She nodded and took a small tape recorder out of a suede bag hanging from a shoulder. "Busy, but not too busy to get a story."

He sat on the bed and gestured to the only chair.

She sat. "I was at your place tonight," she said. "Terrible thing to happen. Did you know Willard Bearclaw?"

"On the record?"

"Does it make any difference?" she asked.

"I guess not, really."

She put the tape recorder on the floor between them. "Okay if I tape this?" He nodded and she punched the "record" button.

"No, I didn't know Willard Bearclaw. I saw him twice. We weren't even introduced. Bobby Whitefish told me who he was, but it wasn't what you'd call a formal introduction."

"I heard about your trouble with him at the Buckskin Mall," she said. "Any comment on that?"

"No comment."

"You and Jack Mink found his body?"

"No comment again."

"Oh, come on," said Erica. "I know you and Jack found the body."

"Then you don't need me to tell you. Anything you want to find out about the case, you ask Skinner," said Jason.

"Anything new on your uncle?"

"That's the sheriff's jurisdiction too."

She nodded, leaned down, and picked up the tape recorder. As she punched the "off" button, she asked, "Are you married?"

She seemed so serious that he couldn't help smiling. "No."

"That's nice. I mean, that first night when we went out, I wondered if you were married."

"But you didn't ask."

She shook her head. "No. Maybe I was sort of getting interested in you. Maybe I didn't want to spoil it by finding out you had a wife in Milwaukee. Maybe it wouldn't have made any difference if you were married, not if it wasn't going to go farther than one date. But if it were, I'd want to know."

"Well, I'm not married. I got close to it about five months ago. After I got shot, she decided she didn't want to be tied up with somebody who might be a cripple. It was a fairly friendly separation. She even gave me the ring back. Turned out the joke was on her. I'm not crippled."

He felt a twinge in his back as he moved his position on the bed and realized he still wasn't completely un-crippled. But now the twinges came only occasionally or when he was tired.

She asked, "How long do you plan to stay in Jackpine?"

"I don't know. I'll go to Milwaukee tomorrow. I have to make funeral arrangements for Uncle Roland. I'll be back tomorrow night, I hope. After that, I don't know how long I'll stay."

He wondered if she could be still interested in him. One way to find out, he decided. He stood up, and so did she.

He said, "Maybe one of these days we can go out again. How does that sound?"

"Fine," she said softly. "For whatever night life we have

here. I haven't heard the Cow Kickers for weeks. They're the ones at the Shantyboy who used to be the Bug Stompers. Every time they get somebody new in the band they change the name."

"Must be quite a bunch," said Jason.

"Hey, you haven't heard anything until you hear country grunge."

"I will, but later, like I said, in a few days. I'm sure you're busy putting out the paper."

"I don't relax until about the middle of Thursday."

He nodded. "Sometime after that, maybe. I'll have to arrange memorial services for Unk Roland in Milwaukee." He looked at his watch. "You feel like a drink?"

"Sure, but just one. That's my limit for a Monday night."

"I promise not to try to get you drunk and seduce you," he said. "Not tonight, anyway. And we'd better have our drink here at the Musky Bar. Do you think it has margaritas?"

"It probably serves whatever the tourists order, but margaritas may be as exotic as fishermen want."

They moved to the door. He paused, wondering if they should go outside. If somebody were looking for him, and that seemed to be what Skinner thought, then it would be safer to stay in the room. But nobody was supposed to know he was at the Musky Manor.

But Erica knew.

Then the window exploded into the room.

Chapter 20

In the Bridal Suite

Jason sat in one of the captain's chairs in front of the sheriff's desk. In the outer office, Erica gave her statement to a deputy. Skinner leaned back and waved his cigar. "When I get busy, I have to smoke. Guess I just can't give up my dog turd." He puffed, then continued, "Lucky nobody was hurt. It was a shotgun, of course. You say there was only one shot?"

Jason shrugged. "I guess. One boom and the glass breaking, near as I remember. It could have been double-barreled shots together."

Skinner said, "We talked to the guy out there, the one at the bar. He had two calls asking which room you were in. One was Erica Chamberlain, of course. He thinks the other one was from a man. Doesn't know who."

"So motor mouth told them where I was."

"He says how the hell was he supposed to know it was a big secret? I told him, but he probably forgot it right away."

Jason recalled the bang and crash together, with him and Erica both frozen for a half second before he grabbed her shoulder and tried to push her to the floor. She was still paralyzed in surprise and wouldn't move. There might have been the noise of a car driving away, but neither of them could hear anything after the shot.

146

Glass glittered like frost everywhere in the room.

Then he heard shouts outside, and someone pounded on the door and asked if anybody was hurt. Next, a city cop had come to talk to everybody. Nobody had seen anything, but everybody had heard the noise.

Skinner asked, "What did you tell Erica about the case?"

"I told her to ask you. I didn't have anything to tell her anyway. I've been thinking about what happened."

"I'll bet you have."

"Maybe it'd be best if nobody mentioned that Erica was with me."

Skinner nodded and sucked on his cigar again. "You're right. But a bunch of people were there last night and saw her. Word'll get around. Hell, we're not so worried about her being in some man's motel room in the middle of the night, not under those circumstances, anyway. But it might be best if whoever shot at you doesn't know anything about her."

"But the bartender said a man called?"

"He thinks it was," said Skinner. "Lots of difference between thinking and knowing. It was sort of in between. Maybe just a soft voice, and the juke box was going loud. You got any idea who might have done this shooting?"

Jason slouched down in the chair wearily. He'd thought about it often enough in the half hour or so since the shooting and come up with no names. There was no hint of who'd killed Willard Bearclaw, either, or even if the same person did the shooting at the motel. Margaret Stuart? She was the only person he'd seen before going to town with Mink that afternoon. He didn't think she felt so insulted that she'd take a shot at him. Possible, but not likely. He decided to say nothing about her, and shook his head.

Skinner said, "You'll have to rough it here for the night. We got a bed made up in the bridal suite. That's the small cell. You'll have it all to yourself. Sorry we don't have jammies and a teddy bear."

"And speaking of them," said Jason, "you didn't give me a security blanket. I was thinking of at least a thirty-eight caliber one."

"We'll fix you up if you want one," said Skinner, "but you'll be safe here. And speaking of jammies, what do you want to do about those clothes?"

Jason looked down at the plastic bag beside him. Inside it, his change of clothing was filled with glass splinters.

He shrugged. "I'll dump them and get new ones tomorrow. Talk about ants in the pants! How about glass in the underwear?"

Skinner called to a deputy in the outer office and told him to bring two cups of coffee. A minute later, he came in and put two steaming cups on the desk. He gave a mock salute and left.

Skinner reached into a bottom drawer and pulled out two pint bottles. "Bourbon and rum. Nothing fancy." He pulled out a stack of plastic glasses, still in their store envelope, from another drawer and gestured to the cans. "Take your pick, I'll have the other. I'm not fussy."

"Bourbon," said Jason.

Skinner poured a healthy dollop of bourbon into the coffees. He raised his cup and they drank a silent toast.

"I'm going to Milwaukee tomorrow. How long will the deputy be staying at the cabin?"

Skinner looked at his watch. "It's not tomorrow. It's today. I'll get a different man out there this morning. Probably Mink. And we'll have other men searching. But we can't keep somebody there all the time. You can't stay there all the time, either. You'll have to come to town to buy food, at least. Somebody wants to kill you. I don't know what we can do to stop it."

Jason again remembered the streets of Milwaukee and the squalid homes where wife-beaters were sure to return to vent their anger and frustration on fearfully waiting victims. And nothing could be done for them; no promises, no protection available, no help, no hope. There was only the certainty that the attacker would return. Most of the victims didn't have the strength or the weapons to defend themselves.

But Jason could have some protection. He said, "Forget the gun. While I'm in Milwaukee, I'll pick up my service piece."

Skinner nodded and stood. "Okay. Come back when you can. If you don't come back, I understand. For tonight, stay here. Have a pizza delivered if you want it."

He looked up as the deputy stood in the open door. "Sheriff, Miss Chamberlain's done. Anything else?"

Skinner waved a hand. "Nothing I can think of. Get the statement typed tomorrow, and she can sign it any time."

Erica stuck her head around the deputy's shoulder. "Jason, I'm headed back to the office. Will I see you tomorrow?"

"I'll be in Milwaukee, like I said. I need to make arrangements for that memorial service down there. It may just be me there."

"I thought the professor would be more popular than that," Skinner grunted as he applied his lighter again to the cigar.

"Most of his friends are dead or so far away they can't come. For somebody who traveled so much and knew so many people, he really didn't have a lot a friends. Maybe it's because he listened instead of talked, so people didn't know much about him personally. And a lot of that listening was research for his writing. Otherwise, he liked to keep to himself.

Writing's like that, he said. Once he gathered his material, he got down to the dull work. Just him and his notes and tapes and typewriter."

Erica asked, "But the people at the university?"

"He didn't get along all that well with them, either. Some of them were jealous. The idea of him making money off writing that sold in popular magazines and books, well, some of the scholarly types thought it was sort of disreputable. You've heard of publish or perish? His colleagues published papers in technical journals or had books by the university presses. They weren't supposed to be profitable. Unk was doing what teachers are supposed to do. He brought knowledge to the public and made it interesting, too. I guess some people in the education business didn't approve of that idea, like people weren't supposed to learn anything unless they paid tuition. Besides, he taught at Madison, and after he retired, he moved to Milwaukee, had an apartment there, and hardly anybody knew who he was. In a sense, he wasn't anybody anymore, not famous, anyway. The magazines he'd been writing for, they folded years ago. Now nobody wants to read about adventure, foreign lands, stuff like that, not when they can see it all on TV."

Jason sighed, took a deep breath, and remembered some of his uncle's opinions. "He said too many of the people he worked with were too pompous, thought they knew everything. He could put up with that for a while just to be polite, but sooner or later he couldn't resist telling them what horse's asses they were. That's one reason he liked it up here. Most of the horse's asses are on horses. I'll have a memorial service up here, too. He probably had more friends here than down there. Anyway, I'll be busy. I'll call you when I get back."

"Fine. I understand."

Jason hoped she did as she waved and left.

Skinner gulped the last of his coffee. "For me, I'm ready to go to bed now. You want anything, ask the deputy. You're not locked in, but you'd better not go out."

Jason nodded, rose, finished his coffee and put the cup on Skinner's desk. Then he followed the sheriff out of the office.

"Sleep tight," said Skinner.

"This isn't the time to say anything about not letting the bedbugs bite," said Jason.

In the cell, he smelled pine cleaner instead of vomit, and thought, for a jail cell, this really was a bridal suite.

He settled down on the cot, then looked at the barred window. He couldn't get out, and nothing could get in but bullets.

He got duct tape from the deputy and taped a sheet over the window, then lay down. After a few drowsy minutes, he decided he was tired enough to sleep. And he was actually alive. He hoped he could keep it that way.

Chapter 21

Satan in the Smoke

Jason sat beside Sheriff Skinner's desk and drummed his fingers impatiently on the top. Skinner sat with his feet on his wastebasket. It didn't seem as if two days had passed. In the outer office, Mink shuffled papers at his desk and the elderly deputy discussed who would have a doughnut break. One difference, Jason decided, was a faint aroma of pizza in the cigar smoke. The spicy smell reminded him that it was after noon, and he hadn't had lunch.

The other difference was with himself. He felt the comfortable weight of the .38 Colt revolver in a belt holster on his left side. The gun was covered by the light sport coat, so he didn't feel so much like John Wayne. An uncomfortable feeling came from the tight collar under his blue necktie. He wore the necktie as an excuse to account for the jacket to cover the gun.

Skinner said, "Nice trip to Milwaukee?"

"Tolerable. I hope my cabin is okay."

"Yeah, it is." Skinner lit a cigar, stared at the glowing end to make sure it burned properly, and continued. "My people are done there, but I've still got Schwartz baby-sitting it."

"Anybody find anything?"

"Nothing that helps," said Skinner. "We been asking

around. Even talked to your old friends, Bobby Whitefish and his pals. None of them knew why Willard was out there, but they think he went back to get his arrow. He'd mentioned that a couple of times, but Bobby didn't want him to go. Didn't want to make any more trouble. Those arrows cost a few bucks, so I guess Willard didn't want to lose it. Went to the cabin when he thought you weren't there. Somebody else was, though."

He puffed his cigar and continued, "And no news on who shot at you. Wouldn't take a Sherlock Holmes to deduce that you wouldn't stay at the cabin after what happened. He— we'll assume it was a he—he'd guess you'd go to a motel. We don't have that many here. He'd just call until he found which one you were in. If he couldn't find you, he'd have to wait for some other time to kill you. At the other motels, no- body who took the calls said the voice sounded familiar.

"You got everything done in Milwaukee? You said you were going to get yourself a gun."

"Yeah, I did. Bigger than that little twenty-two," said Jason. "I've got it on me. I hope you don't mind if it's con- cealed."

Skinner waved a hand through the cigar smoke. "Okay with me."

"I can stay here for a few more days. I made arrangements for a memorial service next week in Milwaukee. I'll have one up here, too. Like I said, he had more friends here."

"And at least one enemy," said Skinner. "After what's happened, I have to assume he didn't shoot himself acciden- tally. And as for Willard, we still don't know if he was killed by an animal or a human, or something in-between."

Jason's eyebrows raised. "In-between?"

"Maybe people have been watching too many horror movies. Crazy monster stories are going around. Of course,

153

the prelim autopsy report on Willard didn't help. I don't suppose you heard about that. Too late to get in the daily papers down south, even if they would be interested in what happens up here in the boondocks."

He puffed patiently on his cigar and stared at the blotter on his desk as if hoping to find some hidden clue. "They still haven't finished the autopsy. Tests on the stomach to make, stuff like that. Reminds me of the old Romans reading the future from the entrails of sacrificed animals. Anyway, we're pretty sure he wasn't poisoned, and they can't tell yet if he was shot, stabbed, or what. Fact is, his chest was so mangled they couldn't tell what did it. There might have been a bullet in his heart, but it's gone. I don't mean the bullet. The heart itself is gone. You might say we found less than expected." Skinner grinned grimly at his humor. "Fact is, some of his chest is missing. Not just chewed up, although there's that, too. I mean the meat was removed, and some of the organs, and a rib or two. They don't know how. Maybe with an ax or knife, maybe by an animal. But it'd have to be a big one, mean and hungry. Doc in Ashland said it was the damnedest thing he'd ever seen. Like somebody butchered him for his tastiest parts."

"Thanks for the appetizing thought." Jason stood and extended his hand. "I'll go back to the cabin this afternoon."

As they shook hands, Skinner said, "Be careful out there. We don't know who or what is running round in those woods. I'll call Schwartz and tell him you're coming."

"It'll probably take me an hour or so," said Jason as he left the office.

As he walked through the outer office, Mink said, "Maybe you should get a dog out there. Something big and growling to warn you, at least."

"The hell with a dog," said Jason. "I don't want something

154

that'll bark all night when it hears a squirrel. Besides, if somebody wanted to kill me, he'd kill the dog first. If I get anything, it'll be a cellular phone."

Mink nodded. "I see your point. Anyway, Erica Chamberlain called this morning. She figured you'd come here first. She left a message she wants to see you."

"Thanks." Jason turned to leave, but Mink's polite cough-like noise caught his attention.

"Mr. Targo, Erica seems to like you a lot."

"We had one date. We went to a movie. That's all."

"None of my business, of course," said Mink softly. "It's just that everybody likes her. We don't want her to get hurt."

Jason said, "We're just friends." He nodded to Mink and left, got into his car and drove the few blocks to the newspaper office.

Damn, he thought when he saw the traffic on the street. I might as well have left the car at the sheriff's office. He parked in the Chamber of Commerce lot and walked to the newspaper office. When he entered, he saw Blanche at her desk. She talked into the phone, saw him, nodded, and pointed toward the inner office. As Jason walked in, Erica saw him, stood and smiled. When they shook hands, he realized he held hers longer than might seem casual. Then, almost embarrassed, she pulled her hand away and sat.

"You're back," she said.

He sat in the chair on the other side of the desk and smiled. "Obviously. Nothing new here, is there? If there is, the sheriff didn't tell me. Or maybe he thinks it's none of my business."

"No," she said. "Nothing new officially, but a guy who writes for the *National Scoop* was here yesterday. The weekly tabloid. I suppose you've seen it in the supermarkets."

Jason nodded. "All the latest news from Atlantis and interviews with Bigfoot. Did this guy talk to the windigo?"

"Probably," she said, also smiling. "Maybe there'll be a picture next week of your cabin burning, with Satan in the smoke. Some people now are whispering about a windigo that haunts your cabin and killed Bearclaw."

"Then maybe everybody will leave me alone out there," said Jason.

"Anyway, some people think you brought all this bad luck."

"Bad luck, hell! Why should they think I'm to blame?"

She shrugged. "You know how it is. They confuse Doctor Frankenstein with the monster. All they know is somebody got killed after you got here. I know, they forget your uncle died before you got here. I just thought I'd warn you."

"Thanks," he said. He remembered Skinner's warning, and his stomach growled as he also recalled the aroma of pizza in the sheriff's office. "Have you had lunch?"

"Yes. Sorry, but I didn't know if you'd be here today at all. Besides, I'm too busy. Give me a couple of days to get the paper out."

"I'll be around," he said. On the way out of the office, he waved to Blanche. She waved back. He thought she didn't act as if he were Doctor Frankenstein. He stepped out to the busy sidewalk. As he looked up and down the street, the faces seemed the same, or more like the same faceless strangers. Nobody stared as if he were some sort of jinx.

He remembered the aroma in Skinner's office and decided to have Italian food. Probably pizza. He recalled the sight of Willard's gutted body and decided against spaghetti.

At the parking lot, he found a sheet of paper on the windshield of his car. He pulled the message out from under the wiper and read it. "GO BACK TO MILWAKEE." There was no black hand, no skull and crossbones, just the four words. He smiled at the misspelling, threw the paper into the back

156

seat, and walked around the car. As he looked at the tires, he also surreptitiously glanced around to see if anyone might be watching him. He saw no one, and the tires weren't flat. He assumed nobody wanted him dead enough to put a bomb in the car. Besides, it was too public in the parking lot. As he started to drive away, he remembered Mink saying something about not wanting Erica to be hurt.

He decided this was more than small town jealousy against outsiders. He wouldn't see her again. Not alone, anyway. Not after what happened at the motel. If he was killed, he didn't want her to die too.

Chapter 22

"Goldilocks Should of Known Better"

At the restaurant, most of the diners ignored Jason. When he paid, the cashier averted her eyes and took the money carefully, as if it might be contaminated by bad luck. At the IGA, where he bought groceries, some people seemed to recognize and avoid him.

He piled the bags of groceries into the passenger seat of the Honda and drove out of town. As he passed the Wilderness of Zin, he noticed someone had stuck the bullet-holed sign back into the ground. After he turned south, he saw the cars ahead on the highway. Damn, an accident?

The cars were parked on the narrow grassy shoulder, some close to the shallow ditch. Several pickups, slewed sideways, partially blocked the road. Only one narrow lane let traffic creep through. As he slowed, he saw a sheriff's car parked on the road to his cabin. He parked behind it and climbed out.

Jack Mink leaned against the cruiser and talked into a radio mike. He nodded to Jason and said into the mike, "He's here now." He paused, then, "All right. I'll tell him." He reached inside, hung up the mike, and turned around. "That was the sheriff. There's a bunch of people here. We can't keep them out, I guess, even though they're really trespassing."

Jason asked, "Why are they here? It's mostly Buckskin land."

"Some of the people around here, not the Buckskins, they decided to go hunting."

"What's in season now?" asked Jason, grinning. "Don't tell me, windigos?"

Mink nodded. "Or lions or tigers or bears, whatever. We got word of this right after you left our office." He gestured toward the road. "George Simpson, he organized it this morning without telling us. Miss Chamberlain got wind of it and called us. We didn't know where you were, except you weren't at the cabin, so the sheriff sent me out here to tell you and to try to keep this bunch from killing each other."

Jason heard a noise behind him, turned, and saw a man in coveralls standing beside the cruiser. The man, short and stubby with a fringe of rust-colored beard, stood with hands on his hips and radiated antagonism. He snarled, "You're Jason Targo?"

Jason nodded. Neither attempted to shake hands.

"George Simpson," said the man. "I've got a resort on the property next to you, and I don't like you coming back up here and stirring up trouble."

Jason smiled. "Me? Seems to me, Mr. Resort Owner, that somebody stirred up trouble for my uncle. And somebody stirred up trouble for Willard Bearclaw and tried to burn my cabin. I don't think I'm stirring up any trouble. And I won't be, unless somebody stirs me first."

Simpson turned to Mink. "You hear that, Mink? He threatened me."

Mink shrugged. "I didn't hear any threat. I heard you making a wild accusation. Or maybe it was slander. And now you've got a bunch of half-cocked guys out here with their guns full-cocked, probably. If somebody gets shot, you'll be lucky if nobody sues you."

"We're making sure everything will be safe," said Simpson.

Jason asked, "You have enough people for a good search?"

Mink told Simpson, "There's plenty of deadfall here, and logs, lots of places for animals to hide. You'd have to check every foot of the area. And you don't even know what you're looking for."

"We're looking for anything big and dangerous enough to kill a Redskin," said Simpson. "And if we don't have enough men, we'll do the best we can with the ones we have."

Jason asked, "Will they be able to see each other as they go through these woods?"

"No, but they'll all be in contact," Simpson answered. "We have cellular phones and walkie talkies, even some CB radios."

"Great!" Mink grunted. "It'll be like people trying to talk to each other in three languages. I didn't see anybody wearing orange hunting jackets."

"Probably safer," said Jason, grinning. "Now they're not good targets. They'll have as much chance as a deer."

An old truck wheezed to a stop on the road. Mink pointed and said, "As if things weren't complicated enough."

Hector Lestray climbed out of the driver's side and Margaret Stuart got out of the passenger's side. Lyle Brennan and Jim O'Kelly jumped out of the bed. Thin Lestray moved like a shadow along the road until he reached the sheriff's car. "Hello, Mr. Simpson," he said. "Thank you for inviting us to join in your hunt. Of course, we have no weapons. We want to make sure the animal you're hunting isn't harmed. After all, our people are friends of all nature, even wild creatures. And yes, I've heard the stories that a windigo has returned."

Lyle stepped to one side, folded his arms, and leaned

against the police car. It sagged under his weight. Although he seemed tough enough to take on a windigo, he quietly watched and listened.

O'Kelly said, "The Native Americans believed in the windigo. We share their beliefs that there are such things, and a windigo could be in these woods. It would be safe, for you and your guns could not hurt it."

"And we don't want your men tramping all over our land," said Margaret.

"We're far enough from your land," said Simpson.

Lestray said, "If you keep going through the woods, no telling where you'll go."

Jason said, "Maybe you should go back to the Wilderness and tell them to stay away. Better not make any noises in the woods, though, or somebody might think you're the windigo." He turned to Mink. "Any of the Buckskins complaining about these guys on their land?"

"Nobody asked permission," said the deputy. "Maybe the reservation police should be here, but they weren't invited. If any of the tribal officials object, they'll have to do it later."

He jerked his head around as they heard, in the distance, three shots. "Shit!" he exclaimed. "Who got shot? Or is somebody lost?"

"Sounded pretty far away," said Jason.

"They walked in about half an hour ago," said Simpson. "They could be a mile into the woods by now. Somebody should be calling in soon."

Everyone froze and listened, as if expecting some other noise, a shot or scream, from the woods.

A new voice asked, "What the fuck are these assholes doing here, Mink?"

Jason turned to find Bobby Whitefish standing beside him.

Mink started to explain, but Bobby broke in with, "They don't have any business on our land. Neither do you, Jason."

"If you mean my cabin, Bobby, it isn't on your land."

"That's right," said O'Kelly. "It's on our land. Hector, we should start making our claim to that land."

"This isn't the time or the place," said Mink. "There might be somebody hurt or killed in those woods. Mr. Simpson, you'd better see what you can find out."

Simpson turned and walked toward the road, where several men stood beside cars and listened to phones and radios.

Mink's radio crackled and a voice said, "Mink?"

Mink reached into the car, pulled out the mike and thumbed the switch. "Here." He turned to Jason. "It's Deputy Schwartz at your place."

Schwartz's voice said, "What's up? I heard shots."

"We don't know yet," said Mink. "Anything going on there?"

"Nothing, except I'm bored as hell. No TV, no radio, nothing to read but old newspapers, and I've read all of them three times. I even read them when they were new."

"It was a bear," said Simpson as he returned. "They can get pretty mean if they're bothered when they have cubs."

"And so one of your guys bothered it," Mink said, sadly. "What about the cubs?"

"Who gives a shit about them?"

Mink snarled, "I do. You don't have any business shooting bears, especially ones with cubs."

"Well, she was attacking," said Simpson. "That's what I heard, anyway. I'll go find out about the cubs." He walked away slowly, as if disgusted that anyone should care what happened to bear cubs.

Mink shouted at Simpson's back, "And get those guys out of the woods!" He turned to Jason. "If the cubs are all right,

I'll bring them to the animal shelter. This sort of thing has happened before. They know how to take care of cubs. You better stay out of the woods until everybody's back here."

Jason shook his head. "You can tell Simpson to let them know I'm coming in."

"Hell, Jason, they're liable to think you're a windigo, or your car is."

"They won't," said Jason. "Can I get past your car?"

"There's enough room to drive around, but I wish you wouldn't go."

"I'll be okay," said Jason as he walked back to his car.

Simpson put cut a hand to stop him from opening the door. "We could settle this the easy way," said Simpson. "I'll buy your place. I could clear the land and add it to my farm, maybe even put another resort there. I don't suppose anybody else would offer much for it, since it's got such a bad reputation now. If somebody makes you an offer, let me know and I'll see if I can top it."

Jason shrugged and nodded, hoping Simpson would be satisfied with such neutral gestures, opened the door and started the car.

Mink waved at Jason as he drove past. Jason thought, Here I come, ready or not. He put a hand on the horn and held it down, blaring as he drove toward the cabin. Now everybody knew he was coming, even the bears and windigos.

Apparently everyone knew, but not everyone cared. He heard a gunshot off to the right, deep in the woods, and saw sparks flash on the hood of his car as a bullet grazed it. He slammed down the gas pedal and the car lurched ahead on the narrow road. In a few minutes, he drove out of the woods and into the parking lot by the cabin. He jammed on the brakes and the car skidded on the gravel to stop with its front bumper a foot away from a sheriff's car. He slumped down on the seat, below the windows, and waited, in case someone else shot at him. Then he slowly raised his head and saw Deputy Schwartz standing in the cabin doorway. He held a revolver pointed upwards, with his index finger outside the trigger guard.

Jason climbed out and waved. Schwartz looked around, then waved back. Jason reached over and picked up a bag of groceries. Schwartz came to the car, looked in, holstered his gun, took the other bag, and followed Jason to the cabin.

As they emptied the bags on the table, the deputy said, "Mink said you were coming, and to hell with nature! I want to get back to TV and civilization and beer."

"You could have had my beers," said Jason.

"This is no place to get drunk and listen to all the strange sounds and think about what happened here. Longfellow was right. The pines do murmur. And I gotta get out of here before I think I understand what they're saying."

"If you're off duty now, you can have a beer," said Jason.

"Thanks. It'll taste good while the posse clears out of the woods."

"When you drive out, use your lights and siren. I had my horn honking, and somebody shot at my car."

Schwartz paused with his finger on a beer can tab. "Accident, you think?"

Jason shrugged. "I don't know. I didn't see anybody. But yes, I think it was probably an accident, a stupid one, like the woods are full of every year in hunting season."

Schwartz pulled the tab and the can popped and fizzed. "Probably," he said, and took a long drink. He licked his lips and continued, "But this time we can't blame it on city slickers. Well, they haven't cornered the market on carelessness or stupidity. You think you'll be all right here?"

"I hope so. After what happened at the motel, I'm as safe here as anyplace."

Schwartz drank again. "I'll check with the sheriff, see if he can't have Mink or me, somebody, come out here to check now and then. But you know how it is."

Jason nodded. "I know. I'll probably go to town tomorrow and see about buying a cellular phone. I'll drop by your office and say hello to everybody."

Schwartz finished the beer, put the empty can on the table and listened. "Radio," he said, and went outside.

Jason saw him talk on the radio for a short time, then he returned.

"That was the sheriff," Schwartz said. "He made a quick decision. The bear did it."

Jason smiled. "Not the butler?"

"The sheriff's story for now is Bearclaw tried to set the fire here. After that, the bear killed him. Skinner says that's his official position unless new evidence shows up. By official, that's what he tells the public, along with a warning to stay away from bears. Hell, everybody up here knows that, or ought to. A mother with cubs, she's no Winnie the Pooh. Even Goldilocks should of known better. Trouble is, out in the woods, you never know when you're going to run across a bear, or vice versa. Anyway, the sheriff hopes that'll shut people up and not disturb the fishermen while we keep on looking. But he doesn't want you to relax and think the bear did it all."

"Yeah. Bearclaw killed by a bear's claw. It's appropriate, but somehow, I don't think that's the whole story."

"Maybe you've forgotten something. The sheriff didn't." Jason thought a moment, then said, "The arrow?"

"Right. It was gone. And Willard's bow wasn't here, so he couldn't have shot the arrow at the bear. It wasn't in the bear,

165

either. If the bear killed Willard, why would it take the arrow? To pick his teeth with? I don't think so."

Jason nodded. "Okay. If anybody asks me who did it, I'll blame the bear. If anybody wants to know who told me, I'll say it was Goldilocks."

Chapter 23

Patience, Hell!

Jason watched Schwartz drive away and remembered Roland had said that the supernatural stuff up here could scare the hell out of anybody. Maybe he just paraphrased Hamlet's line about more things than dreamt of in your philosophy, Horatio. Roland also sometimes had said that the supernatural was just stuff we didn't understand yet. Had Roland been trying to understand something?

Jason took off the jacket, hung it on a nail, removed the tie and tossed it on the bed, then went out the front door and looked to the east. The pines behind the cabin shaded this area, but the lake and trees on the other side glowed brightly. One cloud, like an omen of rain, stretched high in the sky. It was miles away, so fishermen ignored the mushroom-shaped dark thunderhead.

Jason thought that maybe Unk had been working on the supernatural. Roland sometimes talked about how people still believed in ghosts and monsters, even in an age of technological marvels. He'd smile grimly and say, "Science can't tell us how aspirin works, much less why we kill each other."

Jason remembered being with the old man while he studied other cultures, their clothing and houses and economies. But he also learned about their religion, gods, monsters, philosophies. "It's the study of the farthest frontier of all, inside our own brains," he say. "Probably the most supernatural place in this world."

As Jason turned away, he noticed the small desk and the typewriter, now covered by a grocery plastic bag. Roland had carried that old black Royal all over the world. He even typed his notes on it and put them in spiral notebooks for use when he got back to what we call civilization. Civilization? Roland had his own ideas about civilization. He'd say, "The first tool of man is a weapon, so he can kill for territory or a god. Civilization is like a disease, and death is its first symptom."

He opened the books. The mysteries were paperbacks by Agatha Christie. When he flipped through the pages, he found no notes in the margins or anywhere else. The copy of *The True Believer* also had no comments. Roland had never needed a pop philosopher to show him the obvious.

He put the book back on the shelf and went outside. Shadows had begun to creep out over the lake, so the opposite side seemed even brighter. Fishermen in boats were too far away to see the revolver in his belt holster. What else should he think about?

He'd told the sheriff about having a memorial service up here. The library meeting room would be a good place for it. Jason decided to check into that tomorrow, get a cellular phone, and buy stuff to fix the window.

He realized he missed something in the cabin.

Roland's notebook wasn't there. Apparently the sheriff's people hadn't found it. But if they'd missed it, could they have missed something else? On the job, Jason always double-checked everything himself. He decided he'd do that here, too.

He opened the door of the stove, looked inside, and saw the same half-burned wood as before. When he carefully reached in and picked out the top layers, he found more ashes on the bottom, no wire notebook spirals or other metal parts. Nothing under the grate, either. If Roland made notes, where would they be?

He lifted up the mattress and saw only springs underneath. Outside, in the pickup, he found what would be expected, a flashlight with dead batteries, insurance and car registration cards.

Even if Roland hadn't been working on anything, he still would have kept that notebook somewhere, or some notes, even a shopping list.

As he slammed the truck door shut and began to walk back to the cabin, he heard a motor's sputter, turned around and saw Lestray's pickup emerge from the woods. It shuddered to a stop beside the Honda. Lestray waved, climbed out, and walked forward with one hand up, palm out, like an Indian friendship sign.

Jason thought it probably was. He silently waited for the tall man to approach. Lestray pointed to the revolver.

"You think you need that? Yes, I suppose you think you do. But if your enemy is not human, the gun will be useless. You must have faith, as we do, as your uncle did, in the natural spirits which are here."

"Cut the bullshit and get to the point," said Jason.

"Gitchee Manitou is in these trees, this land, this lake," said Lestray. "This is where the hero Nanabozo roamed. This is where the windigo was, and it has returned. But if you will not join our faith, at least allow us to offer you its protection. This land and cabin, we have already said Roland wanted us to have it."

Jason turned and took a step back toward the cabin, but stopped when he heard Lestray's exclamation.

"Wait! Hear me out. I assume you are troubled in many

ways. You were injured, and now recuperate."

Jason faced Lestray and asked, "Why is it you sound like every damn evangelist in and out of jail?"

"All right. I'll use plain language. I want to buy this land. Some of my people think we should go to court to get it, but I want to settle this without spending money on lawyers. We don't have much, but we can scrape up five thousand."

"Go to hell," said Jason, "or go to whatever hell you believe in. You know this land is worth a lot more than five thousand, and I wouldn't sell it anyway, especially to you."

"I suppose you need money," said Lestray, smiling. "I know five thousand isn't much, but it's probably the best offer you'd get."

"Damn it, you aren't listening! No! Now get out of here."

Lestray said, "You probably won't get any other offers for this cursed land, but if you sell us the land and move away, Jason, the curse would be removed, because you are the curse."

"I'll tell you one last time, get out."

"You are in danger," said Lestray. "You should accept our help. If there is a windigo here, we can appease it or drive it away."

Jason walked to the preacher's pickup, stood beside it and pulled out the revolver. "You and your truck are on my property without permission. I'll give you ten seconds to move this or you won't move it anywhere."

"But if you wreck my truck, how will I go away?"

Jason cocked the revolver and pointed it toward the hood. "Walk, run, crawl, swim, I don't care."

Lestray said, "Please consider our offer. My followers get impatient."

The shot sounded like a cannon, and Jason remembered why he always wore earplugs at the practice range. He saw sparks fly off the hood and hoped the bullet ricocheted into the woods without hurting anyone.

"Those old trucks," he muttered, "they had thick steel in those days."

He assumed he said the words, but heard only a loud ringing noise. As he walked to the front and pointed the revolver at the radiator grill, Lestray ran around him, jumped into the cab, and started the engine. He stalled it, restarted it, and backed off, zigzagging in a bluish cloud toward the road. Then he whipped the truck around and drove away through the trees. Jason thought he caught a glimpse of a hand and finger sticking out the truck window.

Jason thought it showed that Lestray was almost human. He grinned, feeling the adrenalin still pounding in his body. He remembered the old cartoon of two buzzards sitting on the cactus. One says, "Patience, hell! I'm gonna kill something!"

It had felt good to do something for a change, even if only to threaten to maim a pickup, but he knew he hadn't solved anything.

Chapter 24

Too Many Nuts and Not Enough Bolts

Jason woke the next morning as the sun shone in his face. He vaguely remembered the familiar dream of the night before, the ice skeleton chasing him, the bullet bouncing along the snowy Milwaukee street. Now he heard putt-putting of motorboats on the lake. He swung his feet off the couch and slowly, carefully, stretched. Last night, he'd read old Jackpine newspapers, tried an Agatha Christie mystery, had steak and fried potatoes for supper and washed them down with a few beers. As he remembered these inconsequential things, he still felt satisfaction from the encounter with Lestray.

A cold washing refreshed and woke him enough to let him boil water for instant coffee. After he drank it, he picked the revolver off the floor and put it in the top dresser drawer. He changed his boxer shorts for swim trunks and walked to the beach. He put a hand above his eyes to shade them from the sun, but it also reflected off the lake. Boat silhouettes floated on sparkling water, and he heard occasional words from the fishermen.

He waded out slowly until he could swim in waist-high water still cool from the night air. As always, he kept away from the boats, even though none were close to shore. He floated and waved at a few fishermen. They waved back. Friendly enough, he decided. Apparently they weren't worried about man-eating windigo monsters. He swam back to the edge of the drop-off and, as he waded back to shore, shook water out of his hair, then brushed it back with a hand. As he neared the cabin, he saw a flash of light against a window curtain. He walked to the north window and peeked inside.

A man stood in the middle of the cabin and pointed a 35mm camera toward the kitchen area. Then the flash illuminated the room as he took another picture. When Jason looked west, he saw a dented red Volkswagen parked beside his Honda. He went back to the east door, opened it, and watched as the man turned and took a picture of him in the doorway.

"What the hell are you doing?" Jason asked.

"Taking pictures," said the man, grinning. He set the camera on the table, held out a hand, and walked forward. "Nesbitt Witherspoon's the name. I'm from Milwaukee, a stringer for the *National Scoop*."

Jason grunted, "That pile of shit?"

Witherspoon was a middle-aged man in a loose, wrinkled suit. His face was also wrinkled, giving the impression of a shar pei in a larger shar pei suit. His wide smile creased a face like a pale prune. "A pile of shit that sells millions of copies every week."

Jason still ignored the outstretched hand. "Why are you taking pictures here?"

"Well, I didn't see any crime scene tape outside, and you weren't here, so I figured I'd get some shots."

"Oh, you're likely to get some shots all right. I might give you a shot on the snotbox."

Witherspoon said, "What's this about a monster? I talked

to some of the people in town and they told me about it, but I want to hear it from you, too. Have you seen it?"

"Who the hell have you been talking to?"

"Oh, all sorts of reputable people."

"Yeah, Turkey Lurkey and Cocky Locky. Get out."

"Don't want to talk about the monster?"

"That's right," said Jason.

"Maybe you're afraid it'll kill you next. Where did the Injun get killed?"

He picked up the camera, walked out the east door, stood near his VW, and turned to take a picture of the cabin. "I hear it was here in front. Come on out and I'll get a picture of you pointing to the spot. Pretty gory sight, wasn't it?"

Jason stood in the doorway and said, "You're on my property. Get out."

Witherspoon smiled again. "Now that there's been a crime committed here, it's public record and all that stuff. I need some quotes from you about how the body was all cut up, or chewed on, or whatever it looked like. I guess the monster is some kind of Redskin Satan, isn't he? What kind of noise does he make? Does he talk to you?"

"Just leave," said Jason, disgusted.

"No comment? That's all right. I'll make you famous anyway. You might even get some money out of this. You know, rights for your story. We don't pay, though. We get enough information without paying for it. And even if you don't talk, that's just as good. We can make something out of silence."

Jason asked, "Haven't you ever heard of invasion of privacy?"

"Like I said, it doesn't apply here."

"Then haven't you heard of decency?"

"This is news, Mr. Targo. Decency doesn't apply there, either."

"How about a lawsuit? Bigfoot or the Martians can't sue, but I can."

Witherspoon shrugged. "Go ahead. Not my problem. We got hordes of lawyers to take care of that stuff. You got your uncle's skull here? I'd like to get a picture of that, too."

Jason felt his body tense and his fists clench. He told himself to stay calm. He'd heard worse than this and not punched somebody. He turned and walked back inside.

Witherspoon shouted, "Yeah, maybe you'd like to get dressed first."

Jason opened the top drawer of the dresser, took out the .38, and brought it to the door. He pointed the gun into the air. "Maybe the windigo looks like you. Maybe I could think you're it. That would be a natural mistake, wouldn't it?"

Witherspoon smiled again, but weakly. "You wouldn't shoot me. I'm a respected member of the press."

"You're a member, all right, you prick! No, I take that back. You're an asshole, and you're not respected even in Milwaukee, I bet. And you're not in Milwaukee. You're up here. If I shot you, I'd probably get a bounty."

"All right," said Witherspoon. "I'll leave, but you're missing your chance to be famous."

He opened the VW door, climbed in, and backed around until he could turn and drive away. He didn't throw a finger. Jason thought maybe somebody had already taught him not to do that.

He went back inside and measured the window frame for new glass. After a shave, shower, doughnut, and another cup of instant coffee, he felt ready to go back to town. He dressed as before, with the tie and light jacket to cover the revolver after he put it on his belt. If somebody saw the lock, maybe he won't bother to look around, might miss the broken window.

★ ★ ★ ★ ★

As he drove toward Jackpine, he remembered that Erica had told him about someone from the *Scoop* nosing around town. He knew he shouldn't have been surprised. He was warned.

As he drove past the Wilderness of Zin, he saw Lestray's pickup pull out of the narrow road and begin to follow. Jason drove at about fifty, passing a few cars and passed by others. The speed seemed safe, for he could usually see ahead far enough to slow for any dangers. Besides, most deer and other wild animals came out at dusk. Once he touched the Honda's brake as a bear, followed by a cub, crossed the road ahead. An oncoming car also slowed. Jason looked in the rear view mirror and saw Lestray's pickup far behind. Even in the distance, Jason thought he could see the old vehicle shake. It didn't seem to be trying to catch up, and probably couldn't no matter how hard the driver pushed the gas pedal. By the time he reached Jackpine, the pickup was out of sight.

Still, Jason mused, was it just a coincidence? Did someone know he would be coming? He had to leave the cabin and go to Jackpine sooner or later, but it seemed like the someone could waste a lot of time waiting for him.

He parked in front of a hardware store on First Street, climbed out, and looked up and down the street. He saw no one he recognized, but knew that meant nothing. He'd found the note on the windshield the day before. He had no idea who'd put it there, but someone must recognize his car.

The hardware clerk gave Jason a long, sideways look, then came to the other side of the counter. "Help you, Mr. Targo?"

Jason nodded. "I need a piece of glass."

"Window glass?"

Jason nodded. He knew if you want everybody to know

something, you telephoned, telegraphed, and they used to say, "Tell a woman," but you could just tell anybody in a small town and the news is spread like pigeon shit in the city.

"Window glass," said Jason. "Single strength will do."

"Sure would," said the clerk. He seemed to infer that even double strength couldn't protect against rocks or bullets.

Jason gave the dimensions, then added, "I need to get other stuff, too, so I can come back later, when it's cut."

" 'Preciate it," said the clerk, nodding. "But it shouldn't take me longer than ten minutes."

Jason nodded and wandered the aisles until he found putty and glazier's points and put them on the counter. The clerk nodded and waved briefly as Jason left the store.

On Second Street, he walked into an electronics store and made arrangements for a cellular phone. "Nothing fancy," he told the clerk. "Just basic service." Again, the clerk seemed to know him. He felt he might as well be wearing a name badge, or maybe an embroidered "A" for "Alien." The clerk said it'd just take a half hour to arrange a phone number for him. Jason paid the deposit, said he'd come back later, and left.

On the street, he heard a wheeze and rattle as the Zinners' truck approached. It stopped in the right hand lane. Big Lyle Brennan seemed to fill the driver's side. He stuck his head out the window and glared at Jason. Lestray got out of the passenger side as Margaret Stuart and Jim O'Kelly jumped out of the bed, then Lyle drove on down the street.

Lestray walked forward and held out a hand. "Glad to see you again, Jason."

Jason marveled at how Lestray could seem to have forgotten yesterday's confrontation. Maybe he'd put it out of his mind. On the other hand, maybe he was a forgiving man. On the third hand, maybe he was a sneaky sleazeball. Jason said nothing, just nodded and put his hands in his pockets. He noticed a cellular phone in a holster on the Zinner's belt. Jason suspected Lestray had somebody watching the cabin, and resolved to pay more attention to the woods there.

Lestray said, "Have you seen anyone about probating your uncle's will?"

"There's a lawyer in Milwaukee who's administrator. He has the will. I have a copy, and there's nothing in it about you or your outfit."

"What a pity," said Lestray. "Our lawyer will be contacting you soon about our claims to the land and cabin."

"Then why are you contacting me now?"

"Just being friendly," said Margaret, smiling. "We want you to understand our position on the rights to the land. We don't want to go to court, but you may force us to do that."

O'Kelly said, "Hector, I told you we shouldn't have done this. We should take care of this in our own way. Our tribal way. There's a windigo on that land, and our only protection is to appease it."

Lestray said, "Anyway, the cabin and land belong to us. You know that all property of our members is shared by all of us. Many of our people could testify in court that Roland was a New Judean. We have a right to our property."

Jason turned away, walked to his Honda, climbed in, and drove to the sheriff's office. Inside, the fan cooled the damp air. Mink looked up and gestured to a nearby chair.

As Jason sat, the deputy said, "Done talking to the preacher? We got a call from somebody at the curio shop on First Street. He wanted to know what we were going to do about having such a troublemaker in town. I asked who he meant. He said you, bringing all these problems, waking up monsters, arguing with religious people, stuff like that. Well, he's a voter, and the sheriff wants us to be polite. I told the guy the guy we don't have jurisdiction on First Street, but thanks

178

for telling us, and I'll call the chief of police right away. I lied. I didn't think you needed any help."

"Thanks a bunch," said Jason, grimacing. "What if that moose, Lyle, what if he'd attacked me? It's all right for me to get beat up, but I'd get arrested if I shot him."

"I didn't think anything would happen on a public street."

"Oh? For all I know, the people are getting their pitchforks and torches so they can chase me to the old mill."

"Then you'll be in our jurisdiction," said Mink. "I suppose you want to know if we've learned anything new about what happened to your uncle or Willard. We've been asking around but haven't learned anything. If more than one person was in on either killing, maybe somebody will squeal, but so far nobody squole."

He rose and walked into the chief's office. Jason heard coffee cup clinks along with Mink's words.

"The Buckskin militants are lying low, too. None of them want us to think they had anything against Willard. He may have been a blowhard, but he never meant any harm, no, not at all, he really was just a peaceful pussy cat with a marshmallow heart. And as for why he was at your cabin, maybe space aliens kidnapped him and put him there. Your old pal, Bobby Whitefish, he's waiting to see what the Zinners are going to do. I think maybe he doesn't want to mess with them."

He returned with two cups of coffee and two doughnuts on a plate.

He continued, "I agree with him. I think you better watch out for Lestray. He's probably more dangerous than the Buckskins. Way things are going these days, if he wants to have human sacrifices, maybe the victims can't complain or they'd interfere with the Zinners' freedom of religion."

Jason nodded. "Roland used to say there's nothing so

weird or disgusting or unbelievable that somebody won't believe it and get other people to follow him."

"That's right. We have strange people running around the streets and woods these days. Years ago, they would have been locked up."

Jason said, "Not only are they not locked up, they're getting interviewed on TV and in the papers."

"So watch yourself," said Mink. "We got too many loose nuts and not enough bolts to hold them."

Chapter 25

The Uninvited Guest

On the way to his car, Jason stopped at the electronics shop, got the cellular phone, looked up the sheriff's department number in the phone book, and called. Mink answered and immediately recognized Jason's voice. "Erica left a message. She wants to talk to you," the deputy said. "She must have heard you're in town."

"I'll go see her," said Jason and gave Mink the cellular phone number. As Jason walked around window shoppers and dodged children, he didn't see anyone else with a phone. The others apparently had come to Jackpine to avoid phones, work, and any worries except if the fish were biting. He picked up the glass, glazier's points and putty and put them on the back seat of the Honda. Then he drove the few blocks to the *News* office.

As always, Blanche sat behind the desk with the phone glued to her ear. "Just a second," she said into the phone, and put a hand over the mouthpiece. "Erica isn't here right now," she told Jason. "She'll be back soon, though."

"I haven't had lunch. Think she could meet me at Muskyville?"

"I don't know if she's had lunch, but I suppose she could go over there to see you. She does want to talk to you."

He saw the headline on the paper lying on the counter. "PROF. TARGO SKULL FOUND, LOCAL MAN KILLED"

He searched in a pocket, found three quarters, put them beside the paper, and picked it up.

"We'll let you pay," said Blanche. "We don't get rich here."

Jason nodded, left the office, and stopped at the edge of the sidewalk. With Lestray, the guy from the tabloid, and who knew how many other nuts in town, Jason decided it would be a good idea to be careful, so he looked both ways and carefully crossed the street to Muskyville. He sat at a table under an umbrella. Other customers stared at him, and he suddenly realized he was the only one wearing a sport jacket, dress shirt and tie. He looked at the menu and, when the waitress came over, smiled and said, "Should I ask what a Muskyburger is?"

"You can ask," she said. "It's just a big hamburger. There's no fish in it, so sue the chef. It's a Muskyburger because we serve it here. And we don't cook the fries in fish grease, so they're good."

"Muskyburger and fries," said Jason, smiling. "I guess my arteries can take it."

She smiled back. "Wisconsin has plenty of fat people who haven't died yet. Something to drink?"

"No thanks," said Jason. As the waitress left, he saw Erica park her car in front of the newspaper office and climb out. He didn't try to contact her, but assumed Blanche would tell her where to find him. He spread the copy of the paper on the table and started to read the lead stories about Bearclaw and the discovery of Roland's skull. The stories were short and, Jason decided, accurate. Erica, or whoever wrote the stories, didn't speculate or make mistakes. There was no need to sensationalize. The facts were lurid enough. He looked up as a shadow fell across the paper. Erica pulled out a chair and sat on the other side of the table.

"I'm having a Muskyburger," he said. "I hope it isn't a mistake."

"It may be, but no one's died from eating one yet. I've eaten, so I'll have coffee and watch you."

He pointed to the paper. "Looks like good, fair stories here."

"It was the best we could do with the facts we had. And the space, too. My slogan is sort of like the *New York Times* one. All the news that fits, I print. Which is why I wanted to talk to you. First, have you made any decisions about staying or leaving?"

"So far, I'm staying."

"Good. I wouldn't want this to be like the end of *High Noon*, where Gary Cooper throws his badge in the dust and rides out of town."

"Well, pardner," said Jason, smiling, "I figger I won't do that, maybe 'cause they's some of the townfolk support me."

"I do," said Erica. "So does Sheriff Skinner and his department."

"I think so. It seems to be more than just professional courtesy between cops."

"You'd better believe it. With Skinner, I don't think there'd be much courtesy if some outside cop came in here and threw his weight around. I've only known you for a few days and this isn't a come-on, but I think you'd be a respectable addition to the town."

Jason grinned. "If that's a come-on, I think it's the weakest one I ever heard. Maybe it's because I'm dressed so respectable today. Well, I ain't no Jukes or Kallikak, but I'm damn sure not as respectable as Lestray and his flock think they are."

Erica said, "He wants to hold a memorial service for your uncle at his place."

"Why the hell should he do it there? Oh, I suppose he thinks it'll support the claim that Roland was a member. My uncle was much too smart to fall for that crap. And I hadn't noticed any signs of insanity or senility in him. Come to think of it, though, I did find one of their brochures at the cabin. It seemed out of place. It's not the sort of thing he would keep, so what was it doing there? I suppose I'll never know. I do know it wouldn't do any good to ask Lestray."

Erica said, "Margaret, you know, what's her boobs, she came to the office a few days ago to get a story in the paper about the memorial service."

Jason opened the paper. "It's in here?"

"Don't bother to look. Not for that, anyway. It isn't there. Blanche called for me, and I turned her down. We didn't have room for it. I'd have to pull the piece on the pick-ups at the shelter, and people here want to get their pets back. She said if I didn't run it, they'd stop advertising. I told her, 'What advertising?' And if she wanted to cancel their subscription, we could grit our teeth and take the loss. Anyway, I wouldn't accept an ad in the personals, either. I said I'd have to check with you first, get your permission. So that's what I'm doing."

"I don't suppose I could stop them. When's the memorial?"

She shrugged, motioned for the waitress and mouthed, "Coffee." The waitress nodded and moved on. "She didn't tell me when," Erica said. "I didn't get a chance to ask, even if I'd wanted to. Margaret was so mad she flounced out. Or maybe I should say bounced out."

"Meow," said Jason, grinning again.

"I know. It sounds like somebody stepped on my tail.

Well, I may have a small town paper, but I don't have to print any bunch of crap somebody hands me. Some papers do, but I won't. Besides, I don't think it would sell any extra copies."

"I've been thinking of having a memorial service too," said Jason. "Some time in the next few days."

She nodded. "Good idea. At least some local people would come, but a notice wouldn't be in the paper until next Wednesday. That gives you plenty of time to arrange a time and place and get the ad in, but maybe you want to have it sooner. You could probably get an announcement on the radio. Enough people listen and the word would spread."

The waitress arrived and put his meal and a cup of coffee on the table. Jason nodded his thanks, paid, and lifted the top of the Muskyburger. Inside, he saw the usual pickle, mayo, and lettuce, but no fish stared back. The fries looked surprisingly dry.

Erica answered his unasked question. "They're not really fries. They're baked."

Between bites, he told her he'd probably try to arrange a memorial service at the library.

"There's a meeting room downstairs," she said. "I think it's spooky, with damp walls like an old wine cellar where you'd expect to find a cask of amontillado. You could probably use it, depending on when it's available." She finished her coffee and stood. "I have to get back to work. Don't worry about the coffee. They never charge me here. Maybe they're afraid our restaurant reviewer would put them out of business. No, we don't have a restaurant reviewer. I never complain about free coffee. Anyway, I wanted to see you again."

She paused, and Jason thought he saw a slight blush in her cheeks. She added, "I mean, tell you about Lestray's memorial service, find out what you were planning, that sort of stuff."

He nodded. "Thanks. I appreciate it. Maybe one of these days, nights, we could get together again."

"I'd like that."

"So would I, but I wouldn't want it to end like the last time we were together."

"That was a little too exciting."

"So don't expect me to call until at least some of this is cleared up. Maybe we should only be together in public."

She nodded again, waved, and walked back to the office. Jason took his last bite of Muskyburger, wiped the mayo off his fingers, followed her across the street, then turned and went to the library.

The librarian seemed familiar. He realized he'd probably seen her that first time, how many days ago? Not even a week, and so much had happened in that time.

When he asked about using the meeting room, she said, "You're late, sort of. Sure, you could use the room, but there's already a memorial service planned for Professor Targo. Not here, though." She pointed toward the front door. "Somebody came in here about a half hour ago and put a notice on our bulletin board, there, by the door."

"Thanks," said Jason. On the board, he saw a hand-lettered photocopied notice. "A MEMORIAL SERVICE FOR PROF. ROLAND TARGO WILL BE HELD MONDAY AT THE WILDERNESS OF ZIN AT TWO PM. EVERYONE IS WELCOME TO PAY TRIBUTE TO OUR LATE FRIEND AND MEMBER."

Jason had just seen the Zinners, and they hadn't told him. Maybe he would be like a third party candidate, the one who wasn't invited to the fancy ball, but shows up anyway just to piss in the punch bowl.

Chapter 26

Last Chance

Jason stopped the Honda at the edge of the clearing, saw nothing suspicious, drove ahead, parked, and slowly walked around the cabin. Finally, satisfied, he unlocked the door and entered. Nothing unusual inside either. He went back to the car and brought in the glass, set it on the table, and went back outside for the glazier's points and putty. He opened both doors, took off his jacket, and felt some relief when a breeze moved through the cabin. He decided against removing the revolver; it felt comfortable on his belt and balanced the cellular phone on his other hip.

The glazier's points held the glass, and he spread a wedge of putty with a kitchen knife. He thought Unk would have approved of the work.

He pulled a can of root beer from the icebox, popped the cap, and sat at the table to think about the future. The future? First, he'd have to think about this afternoon. He sighed and wondered if it had come to this, trapped in his own home. He could go out for supper, but he'd have to expect Lestray to follow him again. Jason thought he could do something about that.

He finished the root beer, put the jacket back on, and went out to the car. He almost had the key in the ignition, then stopped. If he drove away, Lestray would wonder why the Honda didn't show up on the highway.

He put his fingers near the ignition switch, twisted them, silently swore, and set his face in an expression he hoped would show exasperation. He climbed out, opened the hood, and pretended to fiddle with battery cables. In fake annoyance, he slammed the hood down and stared at it for a few moments. Then he shrugged and walked up the road. At the top of the low hill, he turned and looked back. The little cabin seemed a haven of solitary peace, not where bloody death had visited twice.

He walked a few hundred feet up the road, then turned north and silently walked through a dappled green gloom speckled with flickering birds and humming insects. Mosquitoes hovered like small vampires around his face, and he forced himself not to swat at them. He watched his feet as he carefully waded through ferns and around rotten fallen logs. He avoided piles of brush that might cover ravines or hide rattlesnakes, even bears. He tried not to think of the ticks his legs might attract.

After a few minutes he walked more slowly and stopped often to listen and look. He remembered himself and Roland and the Caribs pussy-footing through the jungle with blow-guns, stalking parrots and monkeys. He grinned. If a parrot tastes like chicken, does a monkey taste like an ancestor?

A sound, movement, or some sixth sense stopped him. He stared into the woods ahead and finally saw a large figure rise and stretch. Lyle Brennan looked toward the cabin. Jason waited for, he guessed, five minutes, but saw only Brennan. He spoke softly into a cellular phone, then turned and started to walk toward Jason.

Jason said, "Hold it!"

Brennan jerked and dropped the phone. "Jesus Christ!"

"What'd you tell Lestray? That I'm walking to the highway?"

Brennan picked up the phone and put it into a belt holster. He mumbled, "Yeah. I'm supposed to watch the cabin."

"Why?"

Brennan shrugged. "Don't know. Make sure nothing happens here, I guess, like with the Indian. I'm supposed to tell him when you leave."

"You weren't here this morning. I saw you with him in town."

"We take turns here. I don't mean any harm, nothing like that. I'm just doing like Hector says. It's pretty boring, though. I'd rather be doing something else, even pulling weeds."

"That doesn't sound exciting either."

Brennan grinned. "Nothin's exciting about being at the Wilderness, except maybe the sex. Seein' Margaret's tits when she dances is entertainment all by themselves. Not that I been screwin' her, understand. I got a woman who'd get jealous if I did that. Jesus! I didn't hear you sneakin' up on me."

Jason said, "You've done your job. Want some coffee or a beer?"

Lyle grinned and scratched a mosquito bite. "Not a beer. I don't do that any more. It'd taste good, though. I'll settle for a can of pop. Maybe it'd replace the blood these skeeters been suckin'. Why aren't you scratchin'? Don't you itch?"

Jason moved toward the cabin. "Sure I itch. I just don't scratch."

"I don't know how you stand it."

"I put up with it for ten minutes or so and then it stops itching. If you really have to scratch, try pressing on it."

As Brennan moved through the woods, he pressed one of

189

the lumps on his face. "Hey, I think this works!"

As they entered the cabin, Lyle gave the interior a quick glance. Jason asked, "You've been here before?"

Lyle sat at the table. "Sure. But I didn't try to burn the place down, if that's what you're thinking. We all came here now and then to visit your uncle. He wanted to know what we thought about the Indian religion, our own version of it, stuff like that. I usually said to ask Hector about it. After all, he practically invented it. He runs it. Runs us, too."

Jason opened the icebox. "Root beer all right?"

Lyle nodded. Jason took out a can and said, "Sounds like you're not so happy with Hector."

Lyle took the can, drank deeply, and burped. "Thanks. I used to be Catholic, went to Mass, all that stuff, until one day a priest felt me up. I tried being a Baptist, but they didn't want me to have any fun. I even thought about bein' a Buddhist or Hindu or something but, shit, I don't want to come back as a cow. Not in this country, anyway. Seems like Zin was my last chance. It was supposed to be all love and friendship. It is, pretty much, except nobody loves us but us. We're supposed to be like the Indians, and they hate our guts. It makes me uncomfortable, especially after that run-in with them at the Buckskin Mall the other day. Even if I'm not so happy, I don't know if I could get out. I wouldn't mind going somewhere else but, hell, I don't have nothin'. Not that I had diddly to begin with. Where would I go now?"

"Your family?"

Lyle shrugged and drank again. "They don't want me, now that I'm in this outfit. They're in Arkansas. I don't even know how I could get back there. Hitchhike? I look too tough, don't even have decent clothes. Who'd pick me up?"

He finished the can. "Thanks for the pop. The Prof always gave me some, too. He asked questions, but he didn't even write down the answers. Maybe he wasn't really interested, although he seemed to be. I felt like he was studying us. I'm sure sorry about what happened to him. I don't have any idea who killed him, though, or the Indian, either. You know, it felt good talking, just like it did with your uncle. I don't usually talk much. Hector talks and we all listen."

He stood up and slowly, almost reluctantly, moved toward the door. "I gotta get back to watchin' the place. This was all Hector's idea. If he'd got it before the Indian got killed, maybe one of us would have seen who did it. Hector'd probably get pissed off if he knew I talked to you. He just doesn't want anything to happen to the cabin. Don't know why. It isn't worth a fortune, is it?"

Jason shook his head.

Lyle continued, "If Hector gets the land, maybe he'll sell it, raise money for the Wilderness. Hell, I don't know. He doesn't tell us everything. Anyway, I'll be out there until you go to bed, I guess. Be dull, but I can think about what I'd do if I got back home. If anybody gets close, I'll give a holler."

He waved and walked out the door. Jason went to the window and watched him disappear into the trees almost immediately.

Jason was supposed to feel safe with Lyle watching him, but if the windigo showed up, it wouldn't help if the big guy had left for Arkansas.

He took a steak from the freezer, put it into a pan of water to thaw, then went out the back door and watched the fishermen. He gathered some deadfall and stacked it beside the firepit. He looked at his watch. Three o'clock. He had to find some way to spend the long hours before bedtime.

He went back inside, picked a newspaper from the stack and read it for a few minutes, then went outside again to watch the fishermen. He felt as bored as Lyle, but at least he could leave. He felt some sympathy for the big man. The situation reminded him of childhood friends in other cultures, boys who knew about television, airplanes, and schools. They wanted to learn, maybe even be doctors or educators. They knew the other side of the mountain could be another world, but they stayed neck-deep in a quicksand of culture, family, and strict religion.

Jason grinned and decided Lyle wasn't stuck as much as he thought. He could find help if he looked for it. Even the Salvation Army would welcome him. Jason decided he could give Lyle some encouragement. It might put a kink in Lestray's tail.

He put on the jacket and carried a root beer out the door and into the woods. "Hey, Lyle! I got another root beer. Got some advice, too, if you want to listen!"

He stopped, heard nothing, then moved between the trees.

"Lyle? Lyle?"

This time he heard a faint buzzing to his left, turned and saw Lyle on the ground almost beside him. The buzzing came from a black cloud of flies on exposed intestines spilled into Lyle's lap. His chest and stomach were ripped apart, and his wide eyes seemed to stare at Jason in surprise.

In shock, Jason wondered how such a big man could be so small in death.

He swallowed, swallowed again, and controlled his stomach by looking around for anyone else. Then he remembered to jerk the revolver out. It gave him some comfort, even though he saw no one. He backed away, just far enough to see the cabin, pulled out the cellular phone, and called for help.

He knew he'd have a long wait. He hoped he wouldn't have company before then.

Chapter 27

Bugs on a Board

Death, like Sandburg's fog, had crept in on cat's feet. Had it moved on? Jason sat with his back to a pine tree and hoped it was large enough to provide cover. He held his cocked revolver in his right hand and listened for an animal in the brush, footsteps, a voice, but heard only bird chirps and flies buzzing on Lyle's body.

Finally, Jason heard a motor behind him, then Mink shouting, "Jason?"

"To the north!"

"You okay?"

"Yeah. Be careful. Whoever killed Lyle might still be around."

In a few seconds, Mink appeared through the trees. He stepped slowly, carefully, watching the ground ahead and looking around. His revolver pointed toward the sky.

"The sheriff's here, too. Schwartz is checking the cabin. Doc's coming, and probably Erica Chamberlain. She called just before I left, so I suppose she knows what happened and wants to get all the details."

"Jason, are you all right?"

The new voice seemed tired, muffled in the forest. Jason asked, "Who's that?"

"Charley Rogers."

"How did you find out?"

"I was at the sheriff's office talking to Mink when the call came in. I guess you're all right."

"Better than Lyle."

Charley and Mink moved silently through the forest and stopped in front of him. Mink said, "I guess that nasty old bear is back."

Erica almost bumped into a tree as she ran to Jason. "Are you," and she paused, catching her breath.

"I'm all right. Maybe I should hang a sign around my neck."

"Thank God," she said softly, and seemed almost embarrassed by her concern. She turned and looked at Lyle's body, then swallowed and turned away. "I've seen bodies before," she whispered, "but never as bad as this. You'll never convince anybody this was done by a bear."

"All clear around the cabin," said another voice. Schwartz walked around the tree, looked, and muttered, "Jesus!"

Mink grunted, "Same mess, just like with Willard. Jason, the sheriff probably wants to talk to you."

Jason nodded, rose stiffly, and walked south. Skinner leaned against his patrol car, smoked a cigar, and seemed to look in all directions at once. He waved to Jason. "Any details you can give?"

Jason shook his head. "Lyle and I talked for a while, I gave him a root beer, and he went back out into the woods." He added a brief version of the conversation about Lyle's dissatisfaction with the Zinners, the trip into the woods with another root beer, and finding the body. Then, "I didn't hear any scream or shout, no shot, either."

"Maybe was somebody he knew," said Skinner.

"Or somebody who could sneak up on him. It can be done,

194

even in the woods. Somebody like a good hunter."

"An old-fashioned one. Nowadays, they just stumble around and scare the game, or else they find a good stand and wait for a deer." He grinned. "Then they smoke, a deer smells it and takes off, and the hunter bitches about his bad luck. I can ask Jack or Charley if there are still any hunters around here who could track game and sneak up on it." His head turned toward the west. "And speaking of scaring 'game' . . ." Lestray's truck clattered into the clearing and parked beside Skinner's car. Lestray jumped out, almost shouted, "What happened? Is it Lyle?"

" 'Fraid so," said Skinner.

"Is he dead?"

Skinner nodded again.

Lestray sighed as his shoulders slumped. "I was afraid of that."

Skinner asked, "You were expecting it?"

"He called me every hour." He pointed to the cellular phone on his belt. "Mostly to say he hadn't seen anything. But when he didn't call, I called him and he didn't answer, so I knew something was wrong."

Skinner briefly explained what had happened, and Lestray's face paled as he listened. "My God," he whispered, "poor Susan."

Skinner asked, "His wife?"

Lestray shook his head. "No, but she's been living with him for about a year. I think she really loved him. He was big and kind of rough, but I don't think anybody would want to kill him. I don't know how to tell her."

"Maybe I can help," said Skinner. "I ought to talk to her anyway. We could go to the Wilderness now."

Jason asked, "Okay if I come along?"

"Okay by me," said Skinner.

Jason thought it was a good idea not to ask Lestray.

Lestray drove his pickup to the Wilderness. Skinner and Jason followed in the sheriff's car. They parked beside a few other vehicles in the grassy area and walked to the clearing where the Zinners had sat on logs and watched Margaret dance. Now Jason could see teepees shaded by the pines.

Skinner asked, "Where is everybody?"

"Working, resting, praying," said Lestray. "We don't have rules or schedules."

He led them across the clearing, stopped at one of the teepees, and pulled aside a flap. Jason looked over Lestray's shoulder and saw a woman sleeping on blankets on the ground.

Lestray whispered, "Susan?"

Jason saw another pile of blankets, perhaps where Lyle had slept, and a small dead pine tree stuck into the ground. Clothing dangled limply from the branch stubs. Nearby, a few books leaned against each other on a board across two concrete blocks. Despite the summer heat, a light breeze and the pine tree shade kept the tepee somewhat comfortable.

Susan murmured something, turned, sat up, and rubbed her eyes. She seemed chubby, Jason thought, sort of doughy, although it may have been accented by the puffiness of her sleepy face. She stood up, smiled, and gestured them inside. She wore the Zinners' fake Indian dress costume. Dark hair flowed to her shoulders, and she seemed surprisingly clean, considering the primitive living conditions. She saw the sheriff and frowned.

"We have bad news," said Lestray. "Lyle's had an accident."

Susan gasped and she sat back down on the blankets. She whispered, "Is he dead?"

Skinner nodded.

"Killed," Lestray said quietly.

"Like the others?" she whispered.

Lestray nodded.

She clenched her fists, apparently an effort to repress her emotions. "I knew something like that might happen. Ever since Roland showed up. They were friends, you know, Lyle and Roland."

Skinner asked, "When did you see Lyle last?"

"This morning. He said he was going to go to your place." She gestured to Jason.

"I talked to him," he said. "He said he was thinking of leaving here."

"I know. It was Roland's fault, putting ideas in his head. Roland really didn't think much of the Wilderness, you know."

"You're wrong," said Lestray. "He was one of us."

She shook her head. "Lyle told me the professor was just studying us like we were bugs on a board."

That sounds more like him, Jason thought, but Roland wouldn't say that to his subjects. Maybe age made him cranky.

He averted his eyes and noticed one of the books. Duct tape on the spine matched its dull green cover. He recognized it as Roland's worn paperback $2.50 copy of the abridged *Golden Bough*, James Frazer's classic study of primitive religions. Without thinking, he reached down and picked it up.

"The professor gave him that," she said. "That's part of why Lyle wanted to leave."

Jason opened the cover and saw Roland's signature inside, with no inscription that it had been a gift to anyone. He casually flipped through pages, noticed ball point pen notes in margins and recognized his uncle's writing.

On page 130, he read where Ojibwa Indians seldom cut

living trees, for medicine men said the trees felt the pain. In the narrow left margin, Unk had scrawled, "Acceptable."

On page 406, Jason read about Syrian priests of the goddess Cybele who castrated themselves with swords. And, beside it, in Roland's cramped letters, "Marginally acceptable. They did it to themselves."

On page 503, he read of the Gonds of India, who kidnapped and kept children to be sacrificed to ensure good crops. Unk had written, "An unacceptable insanity." Jason closed the book and gave it back.

He recalled Unk's comparison of religion to old maid sisters who liked pancakes. Somehow, they seemed to be appropriate examples. One sister ate nothing but pancakes three times a day. The second kept trunks full of pancakes in the attic. The third sister obeyed when pancakes told her to kill people.

Susan whispered, "Lyle told me that Roland said all religion is insanity, but it's acceptable until we listen to pancakes. He never said what he meant by that, but even that sounds crazy. Hector, we're not insane, are we?"

"Of course not," said Lestray. "We know the real truth. We're the sane ones."

Susan didn't seem comforted by Lestray's assurances. Jason thought she avoided the subject when she said, "With Lyle gone, will I have to do his work? I suppose so. I've been too lazy."

Jason wondered if that was all the sorrow they showed. Did these people think only of the church, of the work? Lestray also seemed confused by her attitude. He knelt and awkwardly put an arm around her shoulders, as if he wasn't used to such close contact with his followers.

The tent opening darkened as Mink stuck his head in. "I just got here. We haven't found anything special at the scene, so I thought you'd want me to start questioning people here. I brought Schwartz."

Skinner nodded. "Good idea. I got this part done, anyway."

Mink moved back as he muttered, "Better you than me."

Skinner and Jason left the tent. Skinner said, "That's Susan inside. I don't know her last name, but she's Lyle's significant other, or whatever they call them here. She doesn't seem hysterical, so maybe she can talk to you. Usual questions: any enemies, who knew where Lyle was, you know the routine."

Mink nodded.

"I'll go back to the cabin," said Skinner. "Jason, want to ride with me or go back later with Mink?"

"You. I've seen enough of this place, and I want to know what's happening back there."

Skinner said, "Let's go. I worry about my people there with some ripper loose in the woods."

Chapter 28

A Three-Cornered Jigsaw Puzzle

As they drove on the highway, Skinner squinted into the sky and muttered, "Sky's like a sheet of lead pressing down on us. Livid, you know? Lead colored, like a body with the blood drained out."

"I know. I've seen it."

"The Dahmer case? That must have been before your time."

"Thank God. I didn't see it in Africa, either. In Milwaukee, once I saw a hand hooked on a street sign and the rest of the arm, sort of lead-colored, maybe even lard-colored, hanging over a puddle of blood."

Skinner glanced again at the sky. "Wet weather coming. Maybe one of these years we'll have another really bad winter, and I don't know what those Zinners will do. They can get food stamps, so they won't starve, but they might freeze. They expect Lestray to take care of them. Maybe some of them think he's some sort of god, but he can't stop the snow."

As they pulled into the clearing, Jason saw three sheriff's cars, several other cars and an ambulance. Erica trotted to Skinner. "They won't let me take any pictures," she said.

"Won't let you go tromping around, more like it. Besides,

what do you want? A big front page color picture of Brennan's guts? Get a picture of the cabin or use one you shot after Willard got killed. They'll look the same anyway."

She said, "If that guy from the *Scoop* gets here, will you let him take pictures?"

Skinner grinned and pulled a cigar from a shirt pocket. "Maybe, but your paper comes out before his anyway. You'd scoop the *Scoop*. Besides, I think he left town. Maybe the flying saucers finally showed up at that landing field for them down south."

Jason glanced to the north and saw deputy uniforms moving between the trees. A few camera flashes sparkled in the dimness. He climbed out, walked toward them, and stood to watch, hands in his pockets, out of the way, not interfering with the work. Somehow, perhaps because of Skinner's laconic talk and hayseed, cigar-chomping manner, Jason could have expected a sheriff's department of stumblebum yokels, but they seemed competent. And yet, he knew, even the most professional police departments could overlook obvious clues, slide through the routine, or quickly pick the wrong suspect. Even worse in this case, there were no suspects. Each murder had occurred as if in a vacuum, with no witnesses, no clues, no motives.

"Who'd do something like this? Why?"

Jason turned and found Erica standing beside him. He said, "People get killed for a few dollars, a bottle of beer, even a nasty look. Or no reason at all, to us, but there's always a reason. Trouble is, if we can't connect the victims to the killer we can't even guess a reason. It's like a jigsaw puzzle with three corners, maybe a corner missing. We can't find a place to start."

Doc Sanders walked toward them and stopped. "Murder seems to be getting common around here, like a disease.

Better make sure you don't catch it. I'm tired of coming here."

As he walked toward his car, he glared at Skinner, as if the sheriff had caused all this trouble.

Jason felt a drop of water on his shoulder and looked upward. "Want to come inside? I'll make coffee or something."

She shuddered. "It sounds so banal after what happened."

They went inside as a drizzle began to patter the roof. He asked, "Instant all right?" She nodded and he turned on the stove to boil a small pot of water.

She said, "At least nobody tried to burn the place this time. Why would somebody try it before?"

"Maybe somebody wants the lakefront land but not the cabin. Maybe somebody didn't care, just had a grudge against Unk Roland or me."

"I wouldn't want to live here, not after what's happened. Do you still plan to stay?"

He shrugged. "I don't know. I suppose I'll have to go somewhere else to find a job. Maybe back to the force in Milwaukee. Even if I worked in Jackpine, I couldn't live in this cabin for the rest of my life. I'm not that much of a hermit."

The water boiled and he fixed coffee. When he heard a soft knock on the door, he opened it and Skinner and Charley Rogers entered. The sheriff sniffed and grinned around his cigar. "I knew I smelled coffee."

Jason took cups from the cupboard and poured coffee. Indian style, he pointed his chin toward the cigar. "You going to smoke that thing in here?"

"I'll just chew the dog turd." Skinner grinned again, this time at Erica. "Sorry. Private joke."

"Keep it that way," she said.

Charley looked around and said, "I think this is a chair." He reached out, felt the chair, sat, and sighed. "The clouds cover the sun. What time is it?"

"About seven," said Skinner.

Charley sighed again. "It's been a long day already. It's been a long life and I'm an old man. Too old, I think sometimes. My protective grandson isn't here. Do you think I deserve a beer?"

"You deserve a barrel of it," said Jason.

"One can. That is enough to wash away the taste of death I breathed outside. I wonder if there really is a windigo. Perhaps only something like that could do such a thing to that big dead man in the woods."

Skinner said, "Erica, they're getting ready to take him away. Maybe not enough light for good pictures, but go ahead if you want to."

She sipped from the cup, put it on the table, and rose. "I'll get the camera. I'll probably be back before the coffee gets cold."

As she walked out, Jason popped the tab on a can of Leinenkuegel and put it in Charley's hand. The old Indian took a long drink.

"In the old days," he said, "when men thought they were windigos, they killed people, perhaps just the way Willard and this other man were killed. When men went windigo, they ate people, too. I wonder if parts of these two men were eaten."

"Parts of Willard were gone," said Skinner. "The doc said he thinks Lyle's heart is missing. We'll have to wait for the autopsy to be sure. But eaten? Only the killer knows."

Jason asked, "Why now? Men went windigo in the winter, didn't they?"

Charley drank again, then nodded. "Yes, when the cook pots were empty and the spirit of starvation stalked the camp. But now we have food, so no one should go windigo unless there is some other reason. Perhaps some evil man wants us to think he is windigo, or that there is a real windigo here. But even a real one could not be here in summer. His heart and bones of ice would melt."

Jason shuddered as he remembered dreams as chilling as the creature of ice on the frozen lake. "Is the windigo large?"

Charley nodded. "As large as a pine tree. You could see his icy skeleton."

"I've dreamed of him since I came up here. Billy Whitefish and I and the other kids, we played windigokazo. It was a game about a cannibal, but just a game. We didn't know the windigo legend. At least I didn't."

"They learn about it later," said Charley. "But there is no legend of a real windigo here, only of the woman who ate her children and was stabbed with a fish spear."

Jason asked, "That's how you get rid of a windigo? No prayers? No healing ceremony?"

Charley finished his beer, burped, and said, "No. You kill him. In the old days, we poured boiling fat down his throat to melt his frozen heart. But a fish spear works just as well."

Skinner said, "We catch whoever killed those guys, he might not get convicted of murder. He might end up in the state hospital at Mendota for the rest of his life. If I had a choice, I'd rather use the boiling fat. Hell, I'd settle for the fish spear."

They flinched involuntarily as lightning lit the cabin. Jason counted mentally, One, two, three and then, as if in applause, thunder rumbled outside.

Chapter 29

Spirits of Earth, Etc.

Jason sniffed lightning's ozone as Erica and Schwartz entered the cabin. "We did everything we could for tonight," said the deputy. "We even put up crime scene tape. Hell of a lot of good that will do, unless the killer bear can read."

Erica put her camera on the table, sat, picked up her cup, and sipped coffee. "Nothing I can do out there either."

Skinner asked, "Find anything?"

"Nothing useful," Schwartz answered. "Figured we'd all go back to the office."

Skinner nodded. "Me too. Charley, you need a ride home?"

"I'll take him," said Erica.

"Thanks," Skinner said wearily. "I still have a lot to do tonight. Jason, you going to stay here? You could come to town, stay at the motel again or pick a different one. I can even make room in the jail."

"I don't know yet." Jason gestured toward the phone on the table. "When I decide, I'll call."

Skinner rose and touched the brim of his hat. "Be going, then. Best of luck to you."

The others waved or nodded as Skinner and Schwartz walked out, accompanied by a dim lightning flash and another rumble of thunder. Yellow light flickered at the windows as the cars turned and drove away.

Erica finished her coffee and looked at Jason. "Any ideas?"

"Only that this place isn't worth these murders."

Charley asked, "You must ask yourself, is it worth your own life?"

"Not mine. If I give the land back to the tribe, it'll have to fight the Zinners."

Charley nodded. "That's so. Perhaps now the elders would want this land just to keep our boundaries intact and keep out the Zinners."

They jerked in surprise as the south window exploded and a shower of broken glass flew halfway across the room.

"Down!" Jason shouted and yanked the revolver from his belt. Charley and Erica, however, stayed frozen in their positions, except that she brushed at her jeans as if to get rid of shards of glass that hadn't traveled that far. Jason looked at the floor and saw a fist-sized piece of cement.

Bobby's voice from outside seemed close, perhaps next to the window. "Jason!"

Jason and Charley looked at each other. "Shit," said Jason, "it's him again." He moved to the wall, stood beside the window, and shouted, "What do you want this time?"

"Get off our land!"

Jason motioned for the others to get down. Erica slid to the floor underneath the table. Charley stood, felt his way around the table, slowly walked toward the window, and shouted, "You are a disgrace to our people!"

"Who's that?"

"Charley Rogers," the old Indian answered. "And Erica Chamberlain. Are you so cowardly that you'd harm a woman?"

"She don't have any business here. And don't you go

206

shootin' out through the window again, Jason. I got a shotgun. If I see your face, I'll shoot. Throw your gun out the window. Don't try to tell me you don't have one. I been watching you since the cops left and I saw it."

"What if I don't?"

"I'll shoot!"

"He might do it," Erica whispered.

"I don't think so," Jason whispered back, "but let's get this over with." He tossed the revolver through the broken window.

A few seconds later, Bobby opened the front door, entered, and pointed a pump shotgun around the room. "Everybody get away, over there," he said as he gestured with the gun toward the bed. As the others walked to that side of the cabin, he swept everything off the table with the barrel of the shotgun, put it on the table, and sat.

"You are a stupid young man," said Charley as he felt behind him for the edge of the bed and sat.

"Shut up, old fart," Bobby snarled. "You Uncle Tomahawks haven't done anything, so it's time for us to take over."

"Pointing a gun at us won't do any good," said Erica.

"What were the cops doing here?"

"One of the Zinners was killed," said Jason, and then told about Lyle's death.

Erica asked, "Did you kill him with that shotgun?"

Jason shook his head. "I would have heard that. How come the sheriff didn't see you?"

"I came through the woods."

Jason nodded. "Either you're getting quieter or we made too much noise to hear you. What do you want this time?"

"I want your word you'll give my people this land. No, not your word! I want it in writing."

Jason smiled. "Like a treaty with a Paleface? You know

what that's like. Besides, this land isn't legally mine yet. I can't do anything until all the paperwork is done. We sure as hell can't do that tonight."

Charley stood and said, "You forget, young man, this place still is cursed by the windigo."

"We don't believe that shit anymore."

"Maybe you don't, but the tribe does. The elders wouldn't accept the land until the curse is lifted." He pointed a finger at Bobby and intoned, "You never learned the old ways! You don't know how to lift the curse. I do." He sniffed. "I smell tobacco. Give me your cigarettes."

"This is a hell of a time to smoke the peace pipe," Bobby said.

Charley held out his hand. "Tobacco is an important part of all our rituals. Give them to me!"

Bobby took a half-filled pack from a shirt pocket and put it into Charley's hand. "Shit, if it'll make the tribe happy, go ahead with your mumbo jumbo." He looked toward Jason. "Don't you try anything. I'll be watching you."

Charley moved forward, dumped the cigarettes on the table and ripped them open. He leaned close to see what he was doing and then used his left hand to sweep the tobacco into his right palm. He turned slowly around and said, "Spirits of the air, spirits of fire, hear me! Spirits of water, spirits of the earth, hear me!" He held his palm before his mouth and faced the door. "Spirit of the North, hear me!" He gently blew a few shreds of tobacco off his palm. He turned to face Bobby and said, "Spirit of the East, hear me!"

He blew a mighty gust of tobacco into Bobby's face. As the younger Indian recoiled in surprise, Charley reached down, grabbed the shotgun, and swung it. The barrel hit Bobby on the side of the head and he fell sideways off the chair.

Jason leaped forward, grabbed Bobby's arms and knelt on

his back. Jason looked up and smiled. "You got him good, Charley. I wondered about that earth, air, fire, and water stuff."

Charley smiled back. "And he didn't even know west from north. I'm just glad I didn't miss him or shoot somebody, especially myself."

Jason felt the side of Bobby's head and found a bump, but no dampness of blood.

"Still have your handcuffs?" Erica asked.

"No, but I'll make do. Get me a plastic grocery bag from the drawer, will you?"

She did, and he rolled Bobby over on his back, twisted the bag into a rope, and tied it around his wrists.

Bobby twitched, moaned and woke. "What the hell happened?"

Charley grunted, "Heap big Indian warrior got suckered by half-blind old fart Uncle Tomahawk."

"My head hurts like hell!"

"Maybe it'll keep you awake," Jason said. He leaned over and looked into Bobby's eyes. Both pupils were the same size, so Jason guessed there was no concussion. He picked up the shotgun and asked himself, "Is this loaded?" He pumped a shell out and reloaded it, then said, "If you'll be good, maybe I'll let you loose."

Bobby snarled, "Fuck you!"

"Stay tied, suits me." Jason sat and put the shotgun back on the table. "You had a lot of guts when you had the gun on three unarmed people. I got it now. Maybe I'll use it on you. You're the one illegally entering, threatening us, and being a pain in the ass."

Bobby took a deep breath, winced, and finally asked, "What you gonna do now?"

"You want this place so much, maybe I'll let you have it.

Erica and I go to town. Charley goes home. We leave you here to wait for the windigo or whoever killed my uncle and the others. Or maybe you don't worry about that, because you killed them."

"None of us killed anybody! Willard didn't like you, and I know he put that note on your car. Too bad you didn't pay attention and go away, like we wanted. But no, Willard didn't kill anybody, and I didn't kill him. He was my friend."

Jason said, "From what I saw, he wasn't that much of a friend. Well, hell, this place isn't worth even one killing."

Bobby stiffened himself as much as he could, perhaps as a substitute for standing straighter, Jason thought. Bobby said, "All this land was once ours. We should get back what we can, starting with this."

Jason asked, "Did you shoot at us at the motel?"

"Hell no! You think I'm the only one with a shotgun? Besides, when Willard was killed, I didn't know anything about him being here and I didn't know about you being in town. Sure, I found out later what happened. Everybody knew."

"Why would Willard want to burn the cabin?" asked Erica.

"How do I know? No reason we should burn it. It'd make a good fishing cabin the tribe can rent out when we get it back."

Jason said, "I guess it wasn't Willard's lucky day to show up when somebody else came here to torch the place."

Erica looked toward the window as headlights flashed outside. "Who's that now?"

They heard a motor rumble outside, then stop, and the lights went out. "I think it's Lestray's truck," said Jason. They heard a muffled muttering, Lestray's excited voice saying something, then a sharp grunt. Jason picked up the shotgun, moved quickly to the wall, and looked out the broken window. "Don't see anything," he whispered. "The truck, but that's all."

Charley whispered, "Somebody's here."

Jason turned as he heard a faint scratch at the door, like a dog's claws. The knob turned, the door opened a few inches, and a bloody hand reached in and crawled along the floor, as if trying to pull the rest of the body inside. Jason jerked the door open and stared down at Hector Lestray. He rolled over on his back. His mouth opened and shut as he tried to speak, but no sound came out, only bloody bubbles from a deep slash in the throat. His right hand scratched at the floor, but his left hand gripped intestines spilling through a ragged hole in his stomach.

Charley took a step back, hit the cot with the back of his legs and sprawled heavily. He sniffed, swallowed, and whispered, "Somebody's been gutted."

Jason hadn't realized he'd been holding his breath. It whooshed out quickly and then the death smell of coppery blood, bile, and excretion filled the room.

Lestray closed his eyes and mouth, then his right hand fell limply, and his bloody intestines spread to the floor like writhing snakes. His body jerked as a shotgun blast from outside pumped pellets into him. Jason exclaimed in surprise, dropped the shotgun, leaped back and shut the door as far as he could. The bloody left hand, now relaxed, kept the door from latching.

Jason looked at the others. They again were frozen in surprise, but then Charley turned his head slowly toward the east and whispered, "I smell gas, too. And smoke!"

Chapter 30

Déjà vu

The others, stunned to silence, turned their heads when they heard a faint "whoosh." Yellow light flickered outside the east windows.

Bobby struggled to his feet and moved toward the west door. As he started to open it, they heard another shotgun blast and glass from the door's window flew across the room.

"Jesus!" Bobby shrank back. "Are you gonna untie me so I got a chance?" He flattened against the wall. "Look! Even the door's on fire! We don't have a chance anywhere!"

Jason saw smoke creeping under the east door. He knew the entire wall would be burning in a few minutes. "These old pine walls will burn quick. We'll try to get out the back." He kicked the door open. It was on fire, but the opening was clear. "I don't see anybody out there."

Charley stood up and felt his way along the wall as he walked slowly toward the door. "I'll go first."

"No!" Jason grabbed Charley's arm, but the old man shook him off and carefully stepped out the back door. He stood for a second, then turned back and smiled. "I'm still alive. Just point me in the right direction so I don't go into the lake."

Jason took Charley's arm again and they all walked toward

the lake as a slow drizzle dampened their clothing. "The windigo must be waiting for us to come out the other side of the cabin."

Charley paused, gave Jason a questioning look, and kept on walking. "Windigo?"

"He thinks he is."

"People don't go windigo in summer."

"He does if he doesn't know much about them," said Jason. "What he knows is really what he imagines. I think." He felt on his belt. "Damn! The phone is in the cabin." He saw a few boats on the lake, but knew a shout for help could draw the killer's attention. "Charley, anybody live close to the south, by the lake?"

"Too close to cursed land."

"Then we go north. Let's go, quietly as we can."

They turned left, crouching and creeping toward the woods on the north. They paused behind a thick pine and looked back.

"There's a jackknife in my left pocket," said Bobby. "Can you cut me loose?"

Jason reached into the pocket, found the knife, and cut the plastic. Bobby flexed his fingers and reached out for the knife. Jason shrugged and laid it in Bobby's hand.

Bobby asked, "You think it's safe to go this way? The land up there belongs to Simpson."

Jason nodded as he remembered the earlier encounter with Simpson.

Bobby added, "He wants your land. Maybe he's behind this."

Jason shook his head. "I don't think so. Let's go."

As if to urge them on, a flash of lightning struck a tree by the lake and thunder immediately blasted their ears. Erica took Charley's other arm. As they led him through the woods, they brushed aside pine branches that slashed their faces. Bobby cursed loudly as he stumbled and fell. Jason hissed to warn him to be quiet.

"Shit!" Bobby muttered. As he got to his feet, he thrashed around in branches that dumped water on him. "Whoever shot at us must be way back there. If we can find a phone, we can call for help."

They slowly stumbled north until they stood in a meadow of knee-high wet grass. Ahead, they could barely see the outline of an old, swaybacked barn.

"Must be Simpson's barn," Bobby said, "but I don't know where his house is."

They swished through dripping grass as they walked forward. A Dutch door leaned slightly ajar. When Jason tried to pull it open, the bottom half fell off and thumped wetly on the ground. He opened the top part and they entered to find shelter, although rain dribbled through the leaky roof.

"Sit here," said Jason. He pushed Charley down gently on a bale of hay by the door opening.

Charley grinned. "I guess this hay's as wet as my ass, but I don't care." He leaned back carefully against the wall, felt behind him, found a handle, and asked, "What's this?"

"Pitchfork," said Jason. "Maybe it's our only weapon. That and your knife, Bobby." He turned and looked. "Bobby? Where the hell's Bobby?"

"I thought he was behind us," said Erica.

Jason looked out the door. "He isn't now."

He handed Erica the pitchfork. "Take this. I'll go look for him."

Erica said, "To hell with him."

Jason said, "We may need him. You can see out there if anybody's coming. Use the pitchfork if you have to."

She nodded.

He said, "I mean it! You go mushy, you'll be dead!" He reached beside the door and picked up a long-handled tool with four steel hooks like large claws. "I'll take this, whatever it is."

Erica said, "It's a manure hook, city slicker."

He looked out the door, didn't see anyone in the rain, and walked back toward the south. He resisted the temptation to call for Bobby. When he reached the spot where he thought they had left the woods, he paused and listened. At first he heard only the patter of rain and drips from the branches, but then the faint drone of a voice came from the woods.

"Oh hear me, Gitchee Manitou."

Jason turned his head. He couldn't see through the trees, but the voice chanted louder in the same rhythm he had heard before. He moved silently through the wet brush as he followed the sound. In a few minutes, he peeked through branches and saw Bobby on his back, arms out-spread like a crucified Jesus with his chest torn open. Jim O'Kelly crouched beside him and held a bloody piece of meat in his left hand as he cut off a small slice with a large knife.

"Oh hear me, Gitchee Manitou." O'Kelly paused, put the piece of meat into his mouth. His next "Oh hear me" was muffled as he chewed. The front of his brown Indian costume was stained with the blood that dripped from his mouth.

O'Kelly was eating Bobby's heart.

Jason backed up carefully, but hit a branch. The water pouring to the ground sounded like a torrent. He held his breath and heard O'Kelly's chant pause. Then, "Who's there?"

Jason didn't see the shotgun, so he gripped the manure hook, ready to swing if O'Kelly moved. The Zinner looked around, then slowly stood up, stuck the knife into his belt and, with the same bloody hand, pulled a small revolver from a pocket.

It looked like Roland's Ruger.

Jason turned and ran toward the barn. Suddenly winded, he paused to look back. It seemed as if he hadn't gone half a block, but he could no longer see the woods. When lightning flashed over the lake he saw O'Kelly standing, staring toward him. Then blackness obscured everything. Jason ran again, almost crashing into the barn before he saw it.

Erica stood at the door, pitchfork ready.

"It's me," he said. "O'Kelly's back there. He's the windigo."

She frowned. "O'Kelly?"

"Lestray's chief honcho. He killed Bobby."

Charley whispered in the darkness, "And ate him?"

"Ate his heart," said Jason. "He may be headed this way. Is there another door?"

Erica shook her head. "No. I checked."

Charley suddenly stood up and turned his head to the south. "He's coming."

Then Jason heard the chant, gripped the manure fork, stepped out the door, and heard the chant repeated, louder, until suddenly the voice seemed almost beside him in the darkness.

He felt tired of running. He seemed to be back on the Serengeti, playing with the Masai kids, running from a pretend lion, then standing to spear it. But this time, instead of a tree trunk target, he faced a human beast. He reached down, picked up the bottom half of the Dutch door. It was much larger than the toy shields he and the other kids had used. He knew it wouldn't stop a bullet, but it might help hide him.

He peeked over the top of the door and saw a dim, dripping form in the darkness. It didn't even seem like a man, but more like the ice skeleton of his dreams. He rubbed water from his eyes and again saw O'Kelly in the rain. His chant grew louder, then stopped. Jason heard a sharp crack as a spat of fire lit the darkness and he heard a bullet whine over his head. He held his breath and heard closer movement in the grass.

As a flash of lightning lit the scene, rain poured down in a thunderous roar. O'Kelly fired quickly. This time, Jason didn't even hear the bullet as it flew into the night. He recalled the John Wayne movies. Wayne always hit the target with a snap shot. Maybe O'Kelly thought he could too, but it didn't work that way in real life. Jason just hoped O'Kelly wasn't lucky! He crouched behind the door and moved to one side, then stood, held the manure hook in the air and waited.

With the next lightning flash, Jason saw O'Kelly facing toward him. As he began to raise the revolver, Jason threw the manure hook, handle first, as if a real lion stood before him. He heard a solid thunk as the handle hit. O'Kelly groaned, and Jason saw him fall.

Jason moved cautiously forward. O'Kelly sat, holding his left hand to his right shoulder. Jason didn't see the gun and hoped it was in the grass. He grabbed the edge of the door, swung it, and heard it hit something solid. O'Kelly fell and didn't move. With the next bolt of lightning, Jason saw him on the ground with blood on the side of his head.

He jumped in surprise as he heard Erica's voice beside him. "Are you all right?"

Except for his pounding heart, all the energy seemed drained from his body. He sat on the grass and let rain wash over him.

He slowly rose, and smiled when he felt no twinge of pain in his back, "I'm okay," he finally whispered. "Maybe he's dead. I don't care. We can't do anything for him here. Can't even carry him out and take care of Charley too. Let's go."

Chapter 31

Ask a Different Question

The sheriff leaned back in his chair, pulled a cigar from a pocket, stared at it, and put it back. He mumbled, "I'll put off chewing el turdo until you're gone." He looked at his watch. "Jesus! After midnight. It's only been a few hours since you called from Simpson's farm, but I'm pooped. Must be getting old. Anyway, O'Kelly has a bruised right shoulder and cracked skull. Now that we could get a search warrant, we found your uncle's notebooks in O'Kelly's tent. He must have been keeping them, sort of like trophies. We read some of what the prof wrote. Hope you don't mind. Anyway, he was researching a paper he titled 'Religion as *folie a beaucoup*.' Ain't that a nutty name for craziness? When Mink talked to O'Kelly earlier today, he said he'd been working in the woods when Brennan got killed. No witnesses, but everything there was communal, even the shotgun and truck, so nobody could verify O'Kelly's story. That's the trouble with these kinds of cases. Without knowing a motive, nobody or anybody could be a suspect. And he made sense then."

"Mink didn't ask the right question," said Jason, "but then he wouldn't even have known which one to ask. Somebody like O'Kelly makes sense when you ask him a question.

Ask him a question about what he believes in and he cracks open like a coconut."

Skinner nodded. "Now sometimes he thinks he's God. Next minute he's the windigo and he's going to eat everybody. He did say your cabin was a desecration of sacred land."

Jason said, "Charley calls it cursed land."

"Sure, to the Indians, it's cursed. To the windigo, it's sacred. It's whatever he thinks it is. He did try to burn the cabin. When Willard showed up, he got killed and eaten. I wonder what'll happen to that bunch now."

"Not our problem," said Jason. "And pardon me if I don't give a rat's ass."

"You own the land. What'll you do about that?"

Jason paused, thinking, then, "I don't know. The Buckskins still don't want it, and I don't want the Zinners to have it, but maybe I'll sell it to somebody else. I might even rebuild and live there."

"I wanted to ask you about that. How you feeling now?"

"Fine. Hitting somebody with a barn door seems to be good physical therapy."

"Then you're well enough to be a deputy. Be good to have a big city cop here, especially if he knows something about the area. Even if the doc says you're not ready for field work, I can give you desk stuff to keep you busy."

Jason nodded. "I'll seriously consider it. I'm not ready to move back to Milwaukee. I don't know if I ever will be."

"Be glad to have you. It might be more quiet, now our crime wave is over."

Jason nodded and smiled. "Well, I could be tough as hell on those dangerous desperadoes who don't return the video tapes."

Chapter 32

Kill Your God

A month later, Jason and Erica went through the museum at Aztlan, then walked slowly up the highest mound to the kiosk with information about the ruins. While she read, he enjoyed the familiar view of rolling hills, woods, and the meandering Wisconsin River. She turned away from the kiosk, stood beside him on the edge of the mound, and said, "That was a good memorial service. I thought you said hardly anybody would show up."

He shrugged and smiled. "I was wrong. People do remember. They remember Roland at Jackpine, too. I wonder if they'll remember the Zinners."

"It didn't take them long to fold their tents and steal away," said Erica, also smiling. "I hear Margaret has moved to California to start another Wilderness there."

Jason said, "Roland always said there was something supernatural about the lake, but he never told me what it was. Maybe he thought I should discover it for myself. After all that happened there, sometimes I think that piece of land is cursed. But just that part. The fishermen don't seem to notice, except when the fish don't bite."

She thought a second, remembering, then, "When we got out of the cabin that night, you seemed to have some idea of who did the killings."

"They fit a religious pattern. Not the windigo part, though. There was a lot of the Indian religion in the Zinners' beliefs, but O'Kelly himself added the windigo. But in the pattern of some primitive religions, the first victim is the unbeliever. That was Unk Roland."

They walked down the grassy slope. He said, "Next is anyone who threatens the authority of the religion. That was supposed to be me. I think when Willard went to the cabin to get his arrow, then the other belief, the windigo one, took over. So Willard got carved up and partly eaten. It was supposed to be me at the motel, too. But back to the religious part, anybody who loses faith has to die. That was Lyle."

He stopped and gestured to the trees on the edge of the river. "The pines. The pines near the cabin reminded me of the sacred grove at Rome where the King of the Woods was murdered by the man who took his place. It's the next thing you do. You kill the spiritual leader, even your god. After O'Kelly killed Lestray, the windigo psychosis took over. But he couldn't even get that right. It wasn't winter, he wasn't an Indian, and he wasn't hungry, but he did become a cannibal. And here, in the old days, where the mound builders were cannibals, maybe they went windigo. Maybe they got power from eating human sacrifices, maybe they were hungry. We don't know why, we just know that some things never change."

Smiling, she said, "There's one good change, though. You said the ice skeleton nightmare hasn't come back."

"Maybe I killed the dream skeleton when I symbolically killed the other windigo."

He gestured toward a rental truck in the parking lot. "And another change, at least my address. Thanks for helping me move. It'll be tougher taking care of Unk's stuff. Maybe some can go to a museum. I might even start a small one in Buckskin, show off the stuff he collected in all his travels. Maybe I'll work for Skinner."

"That'd be good," she said. "You'd be good."

"I think so. At least I hope I have enough experience to know when somebody's been listening to the pancakes."

"What about the pancakes?"

He grinned and took her arm as they walked toward the truck. "Let's head for Buckskin. You haven't heard the pancakes story. There'll be plenty of time to tell you about that."

Author's Note

For some more information on the windigo (wendigo, whittico, wittico):

"Windigo psychosis: the anatomy of an Emic-Etic Confusion" by Lou Marano, *Current Anthropology*, August, 1982.

"On Windigo Psychosis" by Robert A. Brightman, *Current Anthropology*, February, 1983.

And many other sources.

On the Aztlan mounds:

"Ancient Aztlan," by S. A. Barrett, *Bulletin of the Public Museum of Milwaukee*, Vol. XIII, 1933.

And other sources.

About the Author

ANDY GREGG, a native of Chippewa Falls, Wisconsin, studied at the Eau Claire State Teachers College and the University of Wisconsin. After serving in the Army, he worked for the *Eau Claire State Tribune, Milwaukee Sentinel* and *Albuquerque* (New Mexico) *Tribune.* He has written two children's books, *Great Rabbit and the Long-tailed Wildcat* (Albert Whitman and Co.) and *Paul Bunyan and the Winter of the Blue Snow* (River Road Publications) and, as Andrew K. Gregg, the nonfiction title, *New Mexico in the Nineteenth Century* (University of New Mexico Press and Eakin Press). He has also written short fiction, articles, and several stage plays. He lives with his wife, Fay, in Albuquerque, New Mexico, and frequently visits Northern Wisconsin.